W9-BIF-140

THIS BOOK
BELONGS TO:

1988

Sarah Porzig

Merry Christmas!
Love,
Aunt Phyllis &
Uncle Ken

A LITTLE CHILD'S
BOOK OF STORIES

CHILDREN'S CLASSICS

This unique series of Children's Classics™ features accessible and highly readable texts paired with the work of talented and brilliant illustrators of bygone days to create fine editions for today's parents and children to rediscover and treasure. Besides being a handsome addition to any home library, this series features genuine bonded-leather spines stamped in gold, full-color illustrations, and high-quality acid-free paper that will enable these books to be passed from one generation to the next.

A LITTLE CHILD'S BOOK OF STORIES

COMPILED BY
ADA M. SKINNER
AND
ELEANOR L. SKINNER

ILLUSTRATED IN COLOR BY
JESSIE WILLCOX SMITH

CHILDREN'S CLASSICS
NEW YORK

Originally published under the same title in a slightly different form.

Copyright 1922 by Dodd, Mead & Company, Inc., copyright renewed 1949 by Ada M. Skinner and Eleanor L. Skinner. All rights reserved.

This 1988 edition is published by Children's Classics, a division of dilithium Press, Ltd., distributed by Crown Publishers, Inc., 225 Park Avenue South, New York, New York 10003, by arrangement with Dodd, Mead & Company, Inc.

DILITHIUM is a registered trademark and CHILDREN'S CLASSICS is a trademark of dilithium Press, Ltd.

Printed and bound in the United States of America

Library of Congress Cataloging-in-Publication Data

A Little child's book of stories.

   (Children's classics)
   Summary: A collection of stories arranged under the themes "The Happy Child at Home," "Out-of-Doors," "Grandmother's Nursery Corner," "For Winter Time," and "For the Sunday Hour."
   1. Children's stories. [1. Short stories] I. Skinner, Ada M. (Ada Maria), b. 1878. II. Skinner, Eleanor L. (Eleanor Louise), b. 1872. III. Smith, Jessie Willcox, 1863–1935, ill. IV. Series.
PZ5.L713 1988   [E]   87-38208
ISBN 0-517-65959-X

h g f e d c b a

Cover design by Jesse Cohen

CONTENTS

THE HAPPY CHILD AT HOME

OUT-OF-DOORS

GRANDMOTHER'S NURSERY CORNER

FOR WINTER TIME

CONTENTS

FOR THE READING HOUR

EDITORIAL NOTE

The final section of this book, "For the Reading Hour," includes several stories with religious subjects. It is not the intention of the publisher of this edition to preach, but merely to present a classic of children's literature of the first quarter of this century, in the spirit of the time.

C.B.

ILLUSTRATIONS IN COLOR

PREFACE

In this charming collection of stories for little children, Jessie Willcox Smith has done some of her most captivating illustrative work.

Ms. Smith, one of the finest artists of children's book illustration in the early twentieth century, was, at one time, a teacher of young children. Here, she enters wholeheartedly into the spirit of their enthusiasms, their play, and their sense of wonder, drawing us in after her: a three-year-old is totally absorbed in the exacting job of pouring milk for a hungry kitten; another tot, clad in pink, goes out to play among a shower of apple blossoms; and in "Winter Fun," two rosy-cheeked youngsters in deep blue snowsuits revel in a swirl of snow.

The vivid colors and happy vignettes reflect the buoyancy and variety of the stories in the book and create a sparkling companion to *A Child's Book of Stories*, an earlier treasure in the Children's Classics series also illustrated by Jessie Willcox Smith.

1988   CLAIRE BOOSS, Series Editor

FOREWORD

As a gentle breeze drifts over the countryside and imperceptibly builds up strength, becoming more and more a force to be reckoned with, so this delightful book grows, page by page. Starting simply with the child safe and secure at home, the stories take us, first, carefully outdoors to the back yard, then to grandmother's, then through the pleasures and exhilarating difficulties of winter, and finally arrive at a somewhat disguised but always engrossing lesson in character development.

Ada M. Skinner and Eleanor L. Skinner have done a remarkable job of compiling and organizing stories (and, one assumes, writing many as well) which will appeal to the nursery set; and by choosing to emphasize country life, they have shown their talent for understanding the magical appeal that nature has for our youngest little people. Interspersing the stories with the ever-perfect illustrations of Jessie Willcox Smith and dividing the book into four sections comparable to stages of growth in a young child, they have achieved a finished creation which truly deserves its inclusion in the Childrens' Classics series.

The opening section of the book, "The Happy Child at Home," is a collection of sketches from the microcosm of a child's concerns: family pets ("Bruno and the Kitten"), early responsibilities ("Little Wait-a-Minute"), favorite toys and wished-for toys ("The Story of the Toy Woolly Dog"), baby siblings ("Dorothy May's Birthday Gifts"), and the earliest awakenings of the joy of accomplishment ("Little Teddy"), taught not by a parent (though Grandmother tried) but by nature itself:

"Grandmother's right," said Teddy. "The bee, the robin, and the ant are all hard at work. I'm going to weed the garden before I play."

The stories have all the necessary requirements to appeal to little children.

Repetition;

> "Shearers, will you give me, without fail,
>   A dog with a squeak and a curly tail?"
>
> "Carders, will you give me, without fail,
>   A dog with a squeak and a curly tail?"
>
> "Goatherd, will you...."

"Cotton-pickers, will you...."

"Toyman, will you...."

Personification (and onomatopoeia):

"Bow-wow! bow-wow!

Please take me now!"

says the little dog in "Dark Pony," and each familiar barnyard animal makes the same request.

And there are happy endings...even a little lullaby to go to sleep by.

The second section of the book, "Out-of-Doors," is more adventuresome, as befits the first tentative forays of the child from the nest to the still secure but somewhat invigorating freedom of the back yard. The first tales are introduced in this section. "The Discontented Pig" gently reminds the child again that "Every kind of work has something hard about it"; and that story, along with the eternally popular and wonderful "Tale of Peter Rabbit," are charming refrains of what most children of two or three already know: "There's no place like home." "Two Little Sunbeams" is the first real challenge to the child's imagination and is a gem of a story deserving a permanent place on the roster of classic childhood remembrances.

In the third section of the book, "Grandmother's Nursery Corner," the child is spirited away from home and introduced to the engaging world of simple classic folk and fairy tales. The editors' careful selection of stories appropriate for the very young results in parents encountering many old friends: Tom Thumb; Little Red Riding Hood; Little Boy Blue, and some variations on familiar themes, such as "A Clever Mouse," which takes the story of the Three Little Pigs and turns them into mice. Readers are also introduced to an Aesopian or Kipling-like fable, "Why the Banana Belongs to the Monkey." As in the first section (and in so many good children's stories), the device of repetition, in "Little Tuppens," enables the young listener to proudly and correctly anticipate what is to come. However, the introduction of the words "Once upon a time" reminds us that we are now dealing with stories that are a bit more sophisticated. "The Fairy's Best Gift" is perhaps the most elaborate and sophisticated story in the book. It has an intricate plot more in keeping with a fairy tale by the Brothers Grimm or Hans Christian Andersen. There is a spoiled princess who gets lost and is raised as a goatherd by an old woman, and then, after several years, is discovered by a handsome prince; through her experience, she is transformed from a haughty little girl into a sweet and generous young woman who has learned the lesson of humility. Of course, there is a happy ending!

The "Winter Time" section is a smorgasbord of all that has gone before, but with a winter background for icy, stay-indoors days. There are simple little sketches, stories, and poems as well as more complicated folk and fairy tales, all enveloped in an appreciation of the beauties of nature in winter and the magical appeal of a crisp, sunny, snowy morning.

The final section of the book, "For the Reading Hour," is essentially a deliberate combining of lessons in morality, generosity, and helpfulness, with a touch of history added to expose the child to names like George Washington and Florence Nightingale, which may, in the future, be better remembered for the early brush with them. The stories in this section are, to the child's ear, no different from the ones that have gone before. There are giants and ogres and little children, but they all learn something: they all change in some positive way and end up being happier for the change. The astute parent, however, will recogize the parables for what they are, and will enjoy the subtle mixture of spine-strengthening medicine and a spoonful of sugar.

By the time a parent has finished reading this book to his or her child, the child will certainly be older, if only by a month or two chronologically, but both parent and child will have grown as the gentle wind, stronger. The variety of material and the variety of presentational styles may deftly bring parent and child to an unspoken realization that they have taken a beautiful journey together. What better bonding can there be than the intimate sharing of the joy of discovery shining in a child's eyes and the joy of giving reflected in the parent's eyes? May this book bring you and your child to such a place.

PATRICIA BARRETT PERKINS

Baltimore, Maryland
1988

ACKNOWLEDGMENTS

The editors' thanks are due to the following authors and publishers who have permitted the use of valuable material in this book:

To Frances Jenkins Olcott for permission to use her story "Potato! Potato!"; to Maud Lindsay for her story "Mother's Christmas Present"; to Carolyn Sherwin Bailey and Milton Bradley Company for "The Story of the Toy Woolly Dog"; to Clarence and Margaret Weed for their story "King Frog"; to Ossian Lang for permission to reprint the story "What Was in White Hen's Nest"; to E. Vaile and Donahue Company for the story "The Back Yard Party"; to Dodge Publishing Company for the story "A Christmas Craft"; to Fleming H. Revell Company for the poem "Little Mousie Brown" from "Chinese Mother Goose Rhymes" by Isaac Taylor Headland; to Frederick Warne and Company for the story "The Tale of Peter Rabbit," publishers of the original story; to the World Book Company for the story "The Discontented Pig" from Cather's "Education by Story-Telling," copyright, 1918; to J. L. Hammet Company for "Bennie's Sunshine"; to D. Appleton and Company for "The Ogre That Played Jackstraws" from "The Book of Knight and

Barbara''; to Milton Bradley Company for the story "Little Wait-A-Minute"; to Dodd, Mead and Company for the stories "Why the Banana Belongs to the Monkey" from "Fairy Tales from Brazil," and "The Two Little Sunbeams"; to Cassel and Company, publishers of "Little Folks," for the story "Dark Pony"; to Henry Holt and Company for the poem "Bread and Cherries"; to Duffield and Company for the story "Christmas Gifts" from "The Pearl Story Book"; to Richard Wyche for permission to reprint "How Lazy-Bones Was Cured" from "The Story Hour"; to Frederick A. Stokes Company for permission to use "A Garden Surprise" from "When They Were Children" by Amy Steedman.

THE HAPPY CHILD
AT HOME

BRUNO AND THE KITTEN

"Here is my new kitten, Bruno. Her name is Toodles, and she has come to live with us," said Peggy, carrying a little fluffy ball of yellow up to the big collie watchdog that lay sleeping on the porch.

Peggy put the tiny kitten between the dog's front paws and said, "You must help me to take care of her, Bruno."

But to Peggy's surprise Bruno jumped to his feet and walked slowly away, and when Toodles ran playfully after him, he turned and growled at her as if to say, "I have no time for you."

"I'm afraid they will never be friends, mother," said Peggy one day. "And it's all Bruno's fault. Every day Toodles tries to show that she likes him, and he does nothing but growl at her and walk away."

"I don't believe that he would hurt her, though," said mother. "He simply does not want to be bothered with a little playful kitten."

One morning about three weeks later, Toodles was miss-

3

ing. Peggy brought a saucer of milk to the porch and called, "Come, Toodles, here is your breakfast."

But Toodles did not come.

"Mother, have you seen my kitty this morning?" asked Peggy.

"Yes, she was on the porch trying to play with Bruno a little while ago," said mother. "She must be in the garden."

Peggy ran to the garden calling, "Come, Toodles, come and drink your milk!"

Father was in the garden tying up his tomato plants.

"Have you seen Toodles this morning, father?" asked Peggy.

"She was on the porch trying to play with Bruno a little while ago," said father. "But I haven't seen her in the garden."

Peggy ran back to the house crying, "Oh, I'm afraid that naughty Bruno has driven her away."

Then coming to the porch where Bruno was lying she said, "Kitty's lost, Bruno. You have driven her away. Go and find her, this minute!"

Bruno sprang to his feet and bounded away toward the garden. But he did not stop there. On he hurried to the apple orchard, where he ran in and out among the trees. In a little while he stopped, and pointing his nose upward, he barked and barked and barked.

Peggy, father, and mother all hurried to the orchard; and there on one of the highest branches they saw the little yellow kitten.

"It's Toodles!" said Peggy. "Bruno knew where to find her. But what shall we do? She's afraid to come down."

"Little kittens are good climbers," said father, "but they cannot run down from a height. I'll get a ladder from the barn."

Father brought the ladder and soon little Toodles was cuddling in the arms of her little mistress.

"She ran away because you frightened her. I'm sure of that, Bruno," said Peggy, as Bruno trotted along at her side back to the porch.

"Now drink your milk," said Peggy to her hungry little kitten.

Toodles drank her milk eagerly and all the while there stood Bruno watching her.

Later in the morning, Peggy found Bruno lying on the

rug blinking his eyes; and there, between his front paws, lay little Toodles fast asleep.

"Good Bruno, good dog!" said Peggy, patting him.

Then she ran into the house and whispered to her mother, "Bruno and Toodles are good friends at last. Come and see, mother."

LITTLE WAIT-A-MINUTE

Once upon a time there was a little girl named Bessie whom everybody loved. Her father loved her; her mother loved her; her brothers and sisters loved her. Her uncles and aunts and little friends all loved her dearly.

But there was something she used to do that nobody liked. It was this.

When father came home tired from his work, he would often say, "Bessie, will you run upstairs for my slippers?" And Bessie would answer, "Yes, father, I will, but—just wait a minute. I want to put Dolly to bed."

Sometimes when mother was busy in the house she would call from the door, "Bessie, come in, dear, I want you to help me a little." Bessie would answer, "Yes, mother, but—just wait a minute. I want to finish my little garden."

Sometimes her little friends would call, "Bessie, Bessie, come out to play." Then she would often answer, "Wait a minute." By and by every one began to call her Wait-a-Minute. They almost forgot her real name.

One evening father came home late, and Wait-a-Minute ran to meet him. He kissed her, and put his hand down deep into his pocket. Then he brought out two pink tickets.

"Oh, father, father," said the little girl, jumping up and down, "are those circus tickets?"

"Yes," said father, "they are. If you are ready next Saturday at one o'clock when I come home, we will go to the circus."

He told her about the dancing bears, and the funny clowns. Also, he told about the wonderful ladies who jump through paper hoops while riding on horseback, standing up; and about the giant, and the dwarf, till Wait-a-Minute said, "I'll be ready, father. I'll be ready, at one o'clock on Saturday."

So Sunday passed, and Monday passed, and Tuesday passed, and Wednesday passed, and Thursday passed, and Friday passed, and Saturday came. Wait-a-Minute woke up early.

"Mother," she called, "isn't this the day father and I go to the circus?"

"Yes, dear," said her mother, "if you're ready at one o'clock!"

"Oh, I will be ready," said Wait-a-Minute.

She got up, dressed herself, and had her breakfast. Then she went upstairs to play with her dolls. The dolls' house looked so untidy that she said to herself, "I can't leave it like this." So she took out all the furniture and shook the little carpets and rugs.

Nine o'clock passed, and ten o'clock passed, and eleven o'clock passed, and twelve o'clock came. Her mother called upstairs, "Bessie, Bessie, it's time to get ready." But Bessie answered, "Oh, just wait a minute, mother. I am tidying my dolls' house."

Her mother prepared a nice lunch for her, and put it on the table. She was just saying to herself, "Wait-a-Minute will be late," when the bell rang, and there was father!

"Where's Wait-a-Minute? Isn't she ready?" Just then they heard her coming down the stairs. And the town clock struck *one!*

"Oh, Wait-a-Minute, I shall have to take Harry, who lives across the street. He is all ready to go. I saw him when I passed by." And father went out and shut the door.

Then Wait-a-Minute ran to her own little room, and threw herself on the bed, and cried and cried. At last she fell asleep.

Father and Harry soon reached the circus. They saw the dancing bears, and the funny clowns, the hoop lady, the dwarf, and the giant. But all this time father was wishing that Wait-a-Minute might have been there too.

"Where is Wait-a-Minute?" he asked when he came home.

"Fast asleep on her little bed," said mother. "She cried herself to sleep and has never waked up."

Father went upstairs softly. He found Wait-a-Minute asleep on the pillow. He stooped down and kissed her so quietly that she didn't wake up. Then he went downstairs and had supper.

By and by Wait-a-Minute woke up and stole quietly downstairs.

When she saw her father, she threw her arms around his neck, and whispered, "I'm so sorry, father, I was not ready!"

"Perhaps we shall try again," said father.

At last one evening he came home later than usual, and

Wait-a-Minute ran to meet him. What do you think he put in her hands? Two blue tickets.

"Oh, father, father, are they circus tickets?"

"Yes," said her father. "They are for next Saturday, if you are ready in time."

"Oh, I'll *try* to be ready," said Bessie.

The days of the week passed and Saturday came, and when Wait-a-Minute woke up, the sun was shining brightly.

"Oh, mother, mother," she called, "isn't this the day father and I go to the circus?"

"Yes," said her mother, "if you are *ready* in time."

"Oh, I'll try to be ready," said Wait-a-Minute. She hopped out of bed, and began to dress herself.

After breakfast, she ran upstairs to her playroom. The dolls' house was very untidy. She took out all the furniture and shook the little rugs and carpets.

Nine o'clock passed, and ten o'clock passed, and eleven o'clock passed, and twelve o'clock came.

"Bessie, it's time to get ready," called mother.

"I'll come now, mother," said Bessie. She ran downstairs, and there was lunch spread out on the table.

"It was so good, mother," she said, as she finished.

"Then come, dear, and get ready," said mother, and Bessie ran upstairs.

Hands and face were soon washed, and her hair brushed. "Run and get your best little shoes," said her mother. They were put on, then her pretty blue dress and blue coat and her hat. She was just fastening the last button of her little brown gloves, when the bell rang, and there stood father.

"Well, is Wait-a-Min—Oh, there you are, dear! Come along." She turned to kiss her mother good-by, and the town clock struck *one*.

"Just in time," said her father, as they went down the steps. "Do you know, Wait-a-Minute, I'm going to give you a new name, because you were ready to-day. Can you guess what it is?"

Wait-a-Minute thought; then she said, "No, father. But I don't like Wait-a-Minute. What is the new name?"

"Be-on-Time," said her father gently, "my dear little Be-on-Time."

"Oh, father, I like that name," said Bessie. "I hope I can keep it."

And she did.

THE STORY OF THE TOY WOOLLY DOG

There was once a little boy who wanted, oh, very much indeed, he wanted a little woolly toy dog with a squeak and a curly tail. He had a little rubber toy dog and a little china toy dog and a little wooden toy dog, but these would not go to bed with him at night or walk out with him in the daytime.

So one lovely day when the sun was bright and the birds were singing happily, the little boy started out to try to find a little woolly dog with a squeak and a curly tail.

The little boy went and went and went until he came to a faraway green hill, and on the side of the hill he found an old white sheep, all covered with a warm coat of wool and eating grass. The little boy went up to the sheep and said in her ear:

"Kind sheep, will you give me, without fail,
A dog with a squeak and a curly tail?"

13

Then the old sheep stopped eating grass and trotted down the hill with the little boy to a place by the side of a swiftly running, singing little brook where there were a great many sheep. Here, too, were shearers, cutting off the sheep's wool and washing it white in the water. Then this little boy spoke to the shearers and he said:

"Shearers, will you give me, without fail,
   A dog with a squeak and a curly tail?"

So the sheep shearers cut off the soft wool from the old sheep's back and washed it snow white in the brook and put in into the outstretched hands of the little boy, but they said to him, "Go to the carders and ask them to comb out the wool straight and fine."

So the little boy thanked the shearers and he went on farther to a place where busy machines full of sharp-toothed combs went swish, swish, combing sheep's wool. To the carders who tended the machines, he said:

"Carders, will you give me, without fail,
   A dog with a squeak and a curly tail?"

The carders took the wool and put it in their carding

"Now drink your milk," said Peggy to her hungry little kitten.

Page 5

Little Billy stood on his tiptoes and gathered a handful
of the prettiest blossoms.

Page 20

machines. Presently they took it out straight and fine, and they gave it to the little boy, but they said to him, "You must go to the goatherd who lives in the mountain for a bit of skin to hold your wool."

So the little boy thanked the carders and he went on farther to a high mountain where little kids with teetery, tottery legs jumped from crag to crag beside the goatherd who tended them. And the little boy called to the goatherd:

> "Goatherd, will you give to me, without fail,
>   A dog with a squeak and a curly tail?"

The goatherd went into his little house on the side of the mountain and brought out a little piece of smooth, tough skin. He gave it to the little boy, but he said:

"You must go to the cotton-picker for cotton to stuff the skin."

So the little boy thanked the goatherd and he went on farther until he came to a white, sunny field where the cotton-pickers were pulling off great white cotton bolls and dropping them into their baskets. And the little boy called out to the cotton-pickers:

"Cotton-pickers, will you give me, without fail,
A dog with a squeak and a curly tail?"

The cotton-pickers held out a basket of soft white cotton to the little boy, but they said, "You must go to the toyman and ask him to put together your wool and skin and cotton."

So the little boy thanked the cotton-pickers and went farther until he came to a busy toyman, making dolls and picture puzzles and airplanes and toy automobiles and everything else with which it is pleasant to play, in his noisy, clattering workshop. And the little boy said to the toyman:

"Toyman, will you give me, without fail,
A dog with a squeak and a curly tail?"

"Yes, indeed, I will," answered the toyman.

So he got out his glue pot and his scissors and his hammer and his nails, his glass eyes and his squeaks and his little curly tails. He fastened the wool to the skin and he stuffed the skin with cotton and he very soon handed the little boy a little woolly toy dog.

Then the little boy thanked the toyman and ran home as fast as he could, for he was very happy indeed. He had a little rubber toy dog and a little wooden toy dog and a little china toy dog, but now he had a little woollen toy dog that would sleep with him at night and walk out with him in the daytime. And it had a squeak and a curly tail.

DOROTHY MAY'S BIRTHDAY GIFTS

Every morning as soon as little Billy was dressed he said, "I want to see my baby sister, mother."

And mother always took him to the crib where Dorothy May lay sleeping.

"Sweet little sister," said Billy.

One spring morning mother said to him, "This is Dorothy May's birthday."

"Tell me a story about a birthday, mother," coaxed little Billy.

Mother laughed and said, "First tell me how old you are, little Billy."

"I am three years old, mother," he answered.

"Yes," said mother. "You are three years old. And if Dorothy May could talk she would say, 'I am one year old to-day. I have lived with mother and father and little Billie one year. To-day is my birthday.'"

"I like Dorothy May's birthday, mother," said little Billy.

And in the afternoon when grandmother came she brought Dorothy May a little soft pillow for her crib. Grandmother had embroidered Dorothy May's name on one corner of the pillow cover.

"This is a birthday gift for Dorothy May," said grandmother.

"Tell me a story about a birthday gift, grandmother," coaxed little Billy.

Grandmother laughed because Billy always wanted a story. Then she said, "Dorothy May is one year old to-day. I love her very much; so I made her a soft little pillow for her crib. The little pillow is grandmother's gift to Dorothy May. I shall put it into her crib and say, 'Dorothy May, I love you. Here is a birthday gift from grandmother.'"

"I like Dorothy May's birthday gift," said little Billy.

Then away he ran. He went to a large apple tree in the garden. It was filled with lovely blossoms, pink and white. Some of the branches were so low that they almost touched the grass.   Little Billy stood on his tiptoes and gathered a handful of the prettiest blossoms.

Then he hurried to the nursery.   Grandmother had put her birthday gift into the little crib and Dorothy May was lying there cooing and laughing at mother and grandmother.

Little Billy walked up to the crib and laid his pink blossoms on the pillow near Dorothy May's cheek.

She laughed and cooed and he said, "Dorothy May, I love you.   I picked flowers for your birthday gift."

"I know what Dorothy May would say if she could talk," laughed mother.

"What would she say, mother?" asked Billy.

"She would say, 'Thank you, brother, for a real birthday gift.' "

"I like Dorothy May's birthday," said little Billy.

LITTLE TEDDY

"Come, Teddy," said his grandmother. "It is time to weed the garden."

But Teddy hung his head without saying a word.

"Look!" said the grandmother, "the bee, the robin, and the ant have been working ever since daylight came."

"I'm going to ask them," said Teddy as he ran out into the yard. Along came the bee, buzz, buzz, buzz, flying to a clover blossom. "Wait a moment," called Teddy. "Will you play with me to-day?" But the bee buzzed as if to say:

"Little boy, 'tis very true,
There's work for everyone to do.
Not a moment can I stay,
I'm hunting blossoms sweet to-day."

Teddy watched the bee as it flew toward the sweet peas in the garden.

"There's a robin," said the little boy. "I'll see if she will talk to me."

The robin was very busy carrying little pieces of dried grass and twigs to her nest in the elm tree.

"Wait a moment, Robin Redbreast," called Teddy. "Will you play with me to-day?"

But the robin chirped as if to say:

"Little boy, don't you see
  I'm building in the old elm tree?
  Not one moment can I stay,
  I must make my nest to-day."

And away flew Robin Redbreast.

"I shall find some one else," said Teddy as he walked down the narrow sandy path.

Soon he saw a little ant carrying a heavy load for such a tiny creature.

Teddy looked close to the ground. "Little ant," he said, "Will you play with me to-day?"

But the little ant hurried on and seemed to say:

"I'm as busy as the bee,
  Or the robin in the tree.
  Not one moment can I stay,
  My work must be done each day."

Teddy looked after the tiny ant struggling away with her heavy load through the grass.

"Grandmother's right," said Teddy. "The bee, the robin, and the ant are all hard at work. I'm going to weed the garden before I play."

Then to the little ant and bee,
And Robin Redbreast in the tree,
"There's work for me to do," he said.
"I'll weed Grandmother's garden bed."

POTATO! POTATO!

Once there was a little girl. She lived all alone with her mother in a wee house in the wood.

They were very poor, and did not have much to eat; but the little girl wanted Potatoes every day for every meal. She liked them fried and crisp. She liked them mashed with butter and milk. And, better yet, she liked them baked brown and sweet in the hot ashes on the hearth.

One day her mother said: "My child, I am going to town to buy a loaf of bread. Here is a piece of cheese for your luncheon. There is just one Potato left on the shelf in the cupboard. Do not touch it. It is for our supper." Then she went away.

After she was gone the little girl swept the kitchen floor, made the bed, and fed the pigs and chickens. Then she felt, oh! so hungry! And she ate up all the cheese. But it was not lunch-time yet.

When lunch-time really came, the little girl was so very,

Used by permission of, and special arrangement with the author, and Houghton, Mifflin Company, the authorized publishers.

very hungry that she did not know what to do. She thought and thought about the Potato on the shelf in the cupboard.

"How good it would taste fried!" thought she. "No! I would rather have it boiled and mashed! No! No! It would be perfectly delicious baked!"

And before she knew what she was doing, she ran to the cupboard and got the Potato, and buried it in the hot ashes on the hearth. Then she sat down to watch it.

By and by she heard "Puff! Puff! Puff!" and she knew that the Potato was done.

She was just going to dig it out of the ashes with a fork, when up jumped the Potato himself! He had a mouth, and a nose, and eyes all round him, and spindle legs and arms. He went straight up the chimney and was gone.

Well, the little girl was so frightened that she ran out of the house, and looked up at the chimney. And there sat the Potato on the roof, laughing and holding his sides.

She got a ladder and climbed to the roof. She put out her hand and was just going to catch him, when—*puff!* the Potato was gone again. She looked, and there he was running along the road in front of the house. She clambered down and hastened after, crying and crying:

"Potato! Potato! Come back! Come back!
Or my mother will scold me. Alack! Alack!"

And the Potato called and called:

"Catch me! Catch me! And carry me back!
And you shall have a Magic Sack!"

He ran fast, but she ran faster. She put out her hand, and was just going to catch him, when—*puff!* the Potato was gone again!

Then she heard him laugh over her head. And there he sat on the branch of a tree, laughing and holding his sides.

So she climbed up. She put out her hand and was just going to catch him, when—*puff!* the Potato was gone again!

She looked, and there he was running away through the woods. She clambered down and hastened after, weeping and weeping:

"Potato! Potato! Come back! Come back!
Or my mother will whip me! Alack! Alack!"

And the Potato called and called:

"Catch me! Catch me! And carry me back!
And you shall have a Magic Sack!"

And he ran fast; but she ran faster. She put out her hand, and was just going to catch him, when—*puff!* the Potato was gone again.

Then she heard him laugh near her feet. And there he sat at the bottom of an old dried well, laughing and holding his sides.

She put out her hand, and *caught him.*

Then—*puff!* the Potato was gone again, and what do you think?

The little girl found herself standing in the door of her own wee house.

She ran into the kitchen, and there was the Potato—just an ordinary one again, brown and dirty—lying on the shelf in the cupboard, and near it was a Magic Sack filled with new, clean, pink Potatoes!

And when the little girl's mother came home, she was delighted to find the Magic Sack. And though she cooked a great many of the Potatoes for supper, she could not empty the sack, for every time she took one out another came in its place.

So after that, every day at every meal, the little girl had all the Potatoes she wanted to eat. She had them fried and crisp for breakfast. She had them mashed with butter and milk for luncheon. And for supper she had them, best of all, baked brown and sweet in the hot ashes on the hearth.

BREAD AND CHERRIES

"Cherries, ripe cherries!"
  The old woman cried,
In her snowy white apron
  And basket beside;
And the little boys came,
  Eyes shining, cheeks red,
To buy bags of cherries
  To eat with their bread.

TRIX

Mary lives very near the schoolhouse. Every morning as she starts to school Trix stands at the gate. He watches her go down the road and then into that great building. No doubt he wonders why he, too, can't go there, and why Mary goes every day instead of staying outdoors and playing with him.

One day when Trix looked quite sad, Mary said, "Now, Trix, if you are a good dog, I'll take you to school this afternoon. Not when the boys and girls are there, for that would never do; but after they have gone home. Then you can show my teacher what clever tricks you can do."

Trix was very lonely while he waited for school to close. The time seemed long, and no dog was ever happier than Trix when he saw Mary coming toward home.

"Wait till I get your cap, Trix, for I am going to dress you up," said Mary.

She ran into the house but was soon back. They were

now ready and they started for the school where Miss Norris and some of the pupils were waiting.

"This is my teacher, Trix. I want you to show her what a fine dog you are. Come, now." And Mary tapped her foot on the floor. Trix knew what it meant. In a moment he began to roll over and over. How the children laughed at his funny ways!

"Show them how you can dance," said his little mistress.

Trix stood on his hind legs and turned round and round, while Mary tapped her foot all the time.

"Good little dog!" said Miss Norris. "You deserve something for doing such clever tricks."

"Oh, he can do many more," said Mary. "Come, Trix, jump through our arms." Jane and Mary took hands while Trix leaped through them with one bound.

"That's quite good for such a little dog," said Miss Norris.

"Now lie down and play you are a sleeping dog."

He lay very quietly on the floor and did not move, not even when some one said, "Come, get up." But the word "Ready" from Mary brought him to his feet, wagging his tail as if he, too, enjoyed the fun.

"See, Trix, I have a big piece of candy for you," said Miss Norris.

"That's what Trix likes. We often give him some at home," laughed Mary.

Trix seemed quite happy and no doubt would have stayed much longer; but it was getting late.

"Now we must go, Trix, but we will come again when you learn to do something new," said Mary.

He only wagged his tail. Perhaps that was his way of saying how much he liked going to school.

DARK PONY

Once upon a time there was a pony named Dark. Every night he took little people to Sleepytown.

One night as Dark Pony started off, he met a little boy named Noddy, who called out:

> "Whoa! Whoa! Whoa!
> Please let me go!"

So Dark Pony stopped and Noddy hopped upon his back. And away they went galloping, galloping, galloping. Soon they met a little girl named Niddy, who said:

> "I'd like to go, too,
> Please take me with you."

Dark Pony stopped again and up jumped Niddy behind Noddy. Away they went galloping—galloping—galloping.

By and by they heard a little dog barking:

> "Bow-wow! bow-wow!
> Please take me now!"

So Dark Pony stopped galloping. Noddy jumped down and got the little dog. He tucked him under his arm, and jumped upon the pony. And Dark Pony went galloping—galloping—galloping.

Next they saw a little cat, who cried:

"Mew—mew, mew!
Please take me too!"

Dark Pony stopped galloping. Off jumped Niddy and picked up pussy-cat and held her in her lap. Away they went galloping—galloping—galloping.

As they were passing a farm-house out from his coop flew Mr. Rooster, crowing:

"Cock-a-doodle-doodle-do!
Won't you please take me, too?"

When Dark Pony stopped for Mr. Rooster, he flew up and lighted on Dark Pony's back behind Niddy. And then away they went galloping—galloping—galloping.

When Mrs. Hen saw Mr. Rooster riding away she flew after, calling:

"Cluck! cluck! cluckety cluck!
Take me for good luck!"

Then she flew up behind the rooster and away they went galloping—galloping—galloping.

Pretty soon in the road ahead waddling toward them, nodding his head, came a white something who to Dark Pony said:

"Quack! quack! quack! quack!
Room for me on your back?"

Guess what it was! Yes, a duck! When Dark Pony stopped, it flew upon his back. There was just room for it to sit close up to Mrs. Hen. And away they went galloping—galloping—galloping.

As they were riding through the wood up jumped a little gray squirrel from a tree. He called to them merrily:

"Do look and see
If there's room for me."

Noddy said there was room for one more. So the little squirrel jumped upon Dark Pony. Away they went galloping—galloping—galloping.

A little further on as they were looking down they saw a little quail all dressed in brown. He ran toward them, whistling.

"Bob-White, Bob-White!
May I go to-night?"

Dark Pony was very kind and good and liked to take
as many as he could. But already there were eight passen-
gers. Where to put the ninth was a puzzle.

Finally, Mr. Rooster kindly offered his broad back as
a seat for the little quail, who very gladly accepted it.
And away they went galloping—galloping—galloping.

Pretty soon from the top of a tree flew a big bird as
black as could be. Straight toward them as they rode
along he swiftly flew singing this song:

"Caw! caw! caw! caw!
Is there room for one more?"

Now certainly it did not seem so. But Niddy feeling
sorry for the crow, who longed so very much to go, kindly
to it said: "You may sit here on my head."
But Dark Pony said:

"Oh! no! On my head you may go,
Right between my eyes, you know!"

Sure enough! There was just room for the black crow,
and away they went galloping—galloping—galloping.

What a happy company they were; each one of the ten in his own way, humming a song as they galloped along.

> Soon the song grew soft, and low,
> Slowly now did Dark Pony go.
> Finally, every eye was closing;
> And by the time they all were dozing
> Dark Pony, with head bowed down,
> Passed through the gate of Sleepytown.

COMRADES

"Meow! Meow! Me-ow!" cried the little black kitten. He was such a tiny baby kitten, far too young to be out alone, and here he was wandering along the muddy, rainy road, where the ruts were so high and slippery that he kept sliding down into the puddles at the bottom. His wet black fur stuck so closely to him that it looked like a satin coat, and his blue eyes were as full of raindrops as a hungry baby's are full of tears.

If you can understand pussy language you will understand that all those "meows" meant, "I want to cuddle up to my warm mother, I want some milk, I'm scared and lost and oh dear!"—flop! He went into another puddle. His mother was lying in front of a warm stove with two kittens cuddled up to her, asleep. She did not even notice that her third and smallest baby had been shut out when she and her family came into the kitchen that morning after their usual walk. Some kitten-mothers are not at all like boy-and-girl-mothers, are they?

Trot, trot, trot, came a brown pony down the road and splash, splash went the muddy water from the pony's hoofs and the wheels of the tiny MILK, EGGS, AND BUTTER wagon which the pony drew. The kitten was so spattered with mud that he looked like some brown spotted animal and no pony except a very kind one would have done what the MILK, EGGS, AND BUTTER pony did. He stopped short, making the bottles in the cart jingle together and the eggs shiver for fear they would crack, put his ears forward, and gave a low, soft whinny.

The driver was the kind of man who knows what animals mean, and instead of cracking his whip and crying *gadap*, he jumped out of the cart to see what was the matter. By that time the black kitten was almost scared to death. Right over him was the brown pony's big soft mouth; close behind him were the brown pony's hoofs; and to the black kitten he seemed like a huge monster ready to crush him.

"Whinny, whinny, whinny!" repeated the pony. "Don't be afraid, little chap, we will take care of you," was what he was saying. But the poor kitten, with his ears full of mud, was too stupid to understand and just crouched down in the road, shaking all over.

"Why it's a kitten, poor wee creature!" exclaimed the driver, and although the black kitten was still too scared to understand the words, he understood the warm hands which picked him up and the dry pocket of the rain-coat into which he was slipped.

In front of a blazing fire that evening sat a little boy named Peter. Toys were scattered all around him, splendid toys—a big drum, a music-box, blocks, toy soldiers, and picture books. But in spite of them all Peter was looking very sad. His blue eyes were like the kitten's eyes that morning when they were full of raindrops; but there were no raindrops in that cosy nursery!

"Crackle, crackle, laugh with me!" chuckled the flames in the fireplace. But Peter's lips went still farther up in the middle and down in the corners.

"Master Peter, here's your supper," said Nurse bustling in. "Whatever is the matter with you I don't know. Why don't you laugh and play and eat heartily as you used to?"

She put a bowl of bread and milk on the little table in

front of the fire, and hurried off to talk to the cook about a party they were going to that night when "Master Peter" was asleep.

Through his tears Peter looked at his supper. The gay little flames shone on his silver mug and spoon, making them look as though the fire danced there also. The flames laughed to see themselves shining on the silver as in a mirror! The funny blue ships and Chinese sailors on the bowl of bread and milk, and on the saucer of cookies, shone so clearly in the firelight that the ships seemed to sail and the sailors to run up and down the ropes. On most evenings Peter would have laughed with them, but to-night he felt just as the black kitten had felt in the muddy road that morning, lonely and home-sick. His mother had gone away on a visit, and her good-by present to him had been those splendid toys scattered on the floor.

"They will keep you happy, dear," she had said when she kissed him good-by. But Peter wanted something more than toys to make him happy; he wanted something, somebody, very real for him to play with. There were no children in the neighboring houses, and for the last three days the rain had kept Nurse from taking him to the park where he would have played with Jack and Polly and little Ray.

Peter did not know what made him so sad, but he felt a queer lump come in his throat and in another moment the raindrops in his eyes would have turned into a real storm of tears when—the door opened softly and in walked the black kitten! Then the door was closed quickly by someone outside. Perhaps it was the Milk, Eggs, and Butter Man or—do you think it could have been the Brown Pony himself?

He was the one who had saved the black kitten's life, you know, and who understood all about kittens and little boys, too. Peter sometimes drove behind him with the Milk Man and *once* he had ridden upon his back. So I have a feeling that he had something to do with it.

No one ever *knew* who opened that door, but soon the whole house knew that Peter, sorrowful, tearful, lonely Peter—had found a friend. With a "meow!" of delight the black kitten ran to Peter; and the little boy cuddled it in his arms and fed it milk out of his blue-and-white bowl and scampered gayly around the nursery with it until, happy and sleepy, they rolled up together in a warm ball in front of the dancing flames and went to sleep.

There Nurse found them, and although at first she was not glad to have the black kitten living in the nursery she had not the heart to say so when she saw Peter's shining, happy face.

"Nurse, Nurse, see who has come to play with me!" murmured Peter sleepily. "He must sleep on a pillow beside my crib and eat out of my blue ship bowl, and have the belt of my blouse to tie in a bow around his neck on Sundays! See how he loves me, Nurse, he is purring the way the kettle sings and ——" but here Peter fell asleep again while Nurse tucked him up in his cozy bed with the kitten beside him.

That night, when Nurse had gone to the party, a log fell forward in the big fireplace and one gay flame sprang out and danced up and down before it leaped up the chimney. It lighted up the corners of the nursery and of course it looked for Peter. There he lay, fast asleep, dreaming of his kitten, and there, on a cushion beside the crib, was curled the black kitten dreaming of Peter. The flame shone a little more brightly so that it could peek under the eyelids of the boy and the kitten; there was not a trace of raindrops in one of the four blue eyes, nothing but shining dreams in them all.

The flame was just settling back to skip happily up the chimney when it heard outside a soft "Neigh! neigh!" It was the brown pony jogging home after a late, last delivery of cream, and of course the flame, which understood the dreams of a little boy and a kitten, understood what the pony was saying:

"Good night, dear little comrades," he neighed, "bless you, bless you—sweet dreams!"

LULLABY

Rock-a-by, baby,
Your cradle hangs high;
Soft down, your pillow,
Your curtain, the sky.

LOUISA M. ALCOTT

OUT-OF-DOORS

THE CHILDREN'S SECRET

All summer Ned and Betty played in the apple orchard. Have you ever played in one? Do you know what fun it is to stand under the apple trees when they are in blossom, all pink and white, and to sniff and sniff until—you feel all part of the sky and blossoms and bees and butterflies yourself?

Ned and Betty did that, and then the storm came which kept them indoors for three days, while the wind made the house rock and the rain beat upon the window-panes and the nursery fire was very cozy. The next day the sun shone brighter than ever, as though the rain had been washing it, and when the children ran out to the orchard the wind was playing in the treetops, blowing the petals of the blossoms around like snowflakes. Ned and Betty were quite covered with them!

After that, although the blossoms were gone, the orchard was still the nicest place to play in. The children climbed all the trees, and pretended to ride prancing horses on the boughs. They played king and queen as they leaned back on the limbs which were shaped like thrones; or they were sailors, and climbing to the treetops as though they were masts, shouted, "Ship Ahoy!" over the orchard.

But the most wonderful time of all came on a warm July day when Mother let them take their supper to the orchard, bread and jam and milk in a blue jug. Each had a tin cup tied around the waist, like a cowboy. They took them off and were dividing the milk, pouring half into each cup from the blue jug, when they saw *something* hopping toward them.

"Is it a toad or a mouse?" asked Ned.

"It's a funny kind of bird, I think," whispered Betty. They had put their cups on the grass and both children climbed to the lowest branch of the tree and sat there, half hidden by the leaves. They were not afraid, of course, not in their own orchard, but they were puzzled.

"See, it's drinking your milk!" chuckled Ned. "And now it has upset the cup and is caught under it! Listen, oh listen!"

Surely the children did hear a queer, squeaky little voice crying,

"Oh dear, oh dear! Whatever shall I do?"

"Let's help it," whispered Ned.

"Wait!" whispered Betty, clutching his arm, "Let's see what it *is* first; it might be a Goblin!"

"No!" called the little squeaky voice. "I'm not a Goblin at all; I'm a perfectly good Brownie. If I hadn't tried to drink your milk, and upset the cup, you never could have seen me except as a bird or a mouse or a dry leaf perhaps, but now—look!"

The children peered down and there on the ground, kicking hard against the cup, was a pair of tiny brown legs ending in a pair of pointed shoes, far tinier than acorns.

"Oh goodie! He's a real Brownie," giggled Betty. "And now, Mr. Brownie, if we take that cup off will you promise to stay in your Brownie shape and play in the orchard with us the rest of the summer?"

"Yes, yes!" cried the squeaky voice. "Take it off quickly though, because it's heavy and the milk chokes me— Kerchoo—kerchoo!" And the children heard two funny little sneezes, as funny and tiny as the pointed feet.

The children scrambled down and lifted the cup, and

up jumped the gayest little brown figure, in a pointed cap. His twinkling eyes shone through the milk which covered his face. He jumped right onto Ned's hand and rubbed his face against the boy's blue sleeve until the milk was all wiped off. Then he began to dance, and to sing in his queer little voice,

"I'm the gayest little Brownie who ever danced a jig,
For any work of any kind I do not care a fig.
But I'll play jokes with you children, and all the games
you please,
Until the last red apple has fallen from the trees."

The children laughed and laughed and the Brownie clapped his hands and turned a somersault and came down—upon Betty's shoulder!

From that day until the apples had all fallen the children played in the orchard with the Brownie every day. He slept in a hole in a tree, sucked honey from the flowers, and ate the bits of cookies the children brought him—he never wanted to try milk again. But although he told them many tales of the lives of the other Brownies he would never bring one for the children to see.

"They are all around you," he would say, "under the leaves, among the grass—hopping, jumping, creeping. You think they are toads or field mice, just as you thought I was. If that cup hadn't upset and I hadn't had to show you my real shape you wouldn't have seen me either. See—!" He lifted his cap and—was gone! A small bird seemed to flutter in the grass and then, with a gay laugh, he was back. "I won't forget my bargain," he said. "I'll stay until the last apple falls and then——"

"Oh, what do you do then?" cried Betty.

The Brownie stood on tiptoe and whispered in her ear,

"When Jack Frost paints the world all silver,
　　When his mother spreads her quilt of snow,
All leaves and birds and brown things gather
　　In the land of Brownies—where?—who knows!"

"But," he added to both of them, "I'll be near you sometimes even if you can't see me; you may even hear me laugh when you eat your last apple at Christmas time. But look here, these apples are crying out for you to come and pick them up. I'll help you fill that big basket the gardener left."

"How can you help?" asked Betty. "You're only as high as an apple yourself."

"Listen," answered the Brownie. "I've told you many things which seem like magic to you, but are as easy as hopping to us. I've known apple trees ever since I was born in an apple seed and rocked to sleep in an apple blossom. Just close your eyes a moment and listen."

As the children obeyed him they heard the Brownie singing, in such a sleepy voice they couldn't have opened their eyes any more than if the Sand Man had closed them;

"Blossoms and sunshine and warmth and bees
   Helped you to grow on the apple trees,
   Now help yourselves, with the Brownies' powers,
   And jump to the basket like great red flowers
   Blown by the wind—so—jump!"

And when the children jumped too, and opened their eyes, they found the basket filled with fine red apples!

And so they carried them home. (Did the Brownie hide among the apples and help to carry them, I wonder?) And Mother could hardly believe her eyes.

"What wonderful apples!" she exclaimed. "I have

never seen such perfect ones! And to think that you children picked them all up and carried that heavy basket from the orchard yourselves!"

The children looked—as they look in the picture—very shy. They couldn't tell how the apples had been picked without talking about the Brownie and they had an idea he might not like to be talked about. But Mother smiled at them with a twinkle in her eyes as though she understood. Some mothers are as full of magic as Brownies, I think!

Did Ned and Betty ever see the Brownie again? I am sure they did, and played jokes with him; but whether he took the shape of a bird or a mouse, or even a brown puppy or a kitten during the winter days in the nursery, I don't know. You will have to ask the children!

KING FROG

Once upon a time two little boys named Jimmy and Johnny were walking in a field in which there was a pond. When they came near the pond they saw that it was covered with little green water lily pads. In the middle of the pond there was a great, big, green water lily pad. When they came still nearer they saw that on the great, big, green lily pad there was a great, big, green King Frog. On each of the little green lily pads there was a little green frog.

"Oh, Jimmy," said Johnny, "see the great, big, King Frog on the great, big, green lily pad."

"Yes," said Johnny, "and see all the little green frogs on the little green lily pads."

"Let's see if we can hit the great, big, green King Frog with a stone," said Jimmy.

"All right," said Johnny. "Here we go."

Each of the little boys picked up a stone and threw it at the great, big, green King Frog. One stone hit the water on one side of him, and the other hit the water on the other side of him.

"Ker-Choog, Ker-Choog," said the great, big, green King Frog.

"Ker-choog, ker-choog, ker-choog," said all the little green frogs.

"Hear them scolding," said one of the boys. "Let's try again."

"All right," said the other. "Here we go."

As they stooped down to pick up some stones they heard the great, big, green King Frog go hoppity-splash, hoppity-splash over the lily pads toward the shore. At the same time all the little green frogs went hoppity-splash, hoppity-splash over the lily pads toward the shore.

"They're coming after us, Jimmy," said Johnny. "Let's run."

"All right," said Jimmy. "Here we go."

And they ran as fast as they could toward the stone wall beside the road.

After them came the great, big, green King Frog and all the little green frogs going hoppity-jump, hoppity-jump as fast as they could.

When the boys came to the wall they climbed quickly over and ran toward home.

When the frogs came to the wall the great, big, green King Frog jumped easily over. But it was so high that the little green frogs could not jump over.

When the great, big, green King Frog found that the little green frogs had not jumped over, he jumped back.

"What's the matter?" he asked. "Why don't you jump over?"

"The wall is too high—the wall is too high," croaked all the little green frogs together.

"Climb on my back, and I'll take you over," said the great, big, green King Frog. All the little green frogs climbed on the back of the great, big, green King Frog, and he jumped over the wall with them.

All started after the boys—hoppity-jump, hoppity-jump, as fast as they could go.

The boys reached home. As they went in the door they saw all the frogs coming after them. They ran into the house and told their mother that all the frogs were coming after them. She ran to the window and there, sure enough, the frogs were coming up the road, hoppity-jump, hoppity-jump as fast as they could.

When the frogs came to the house, they jumped up on the porch. The great, big, green King Frog knocked upon the door with his front feet. The boys' mother opened the door.

"How do you do, Mr. King Frog? How do you do, all you little green frogs?"

"Pretty well, thank you," said the great, big, green King Frog.

"Pretty well, thank you," said all the little green frogs.

Then the great, big, green King Frog told the lady that two little boys had been throwing stones at them.

"Tell them," said the great, big, green King Frog, "that it hurts frogs just as much to be hit by a stone as it hurts little boys to be hit by a club."

"Dear me," said the lady, "I will surely tell them. Thank you for letting me know."

"Good day," said the great, big, green King Frog.

"Good day," said all the little green frogs.

"Good day to you, Mr. King Frog and all you little green frogs," said the lady.

Then the great, big, green King Frog and all the little green frogs went hoppity-jump down the steps and out into the road and down the road to the stone wall. There all the little green frogs climbed upon the back of the great, big, green King Frog and went over the wall with him. Once more they all went—hoppity-jump, hoppity-jump back to the lily pads, and there they lived happily ever after.

When Johnny and Jimmy saw the great, big, green King Frog and all the little green frogs going down the road and over the stone wall to the green lily pads each little boy saw the round face of the other little boy turn very red.

"Oh, Johnny," said Jimmy, "let's never throw stones at frogs any more."

And they never did.

WHAT WAS IN WHITE HEN'S NEST?

White Hen was on her nest. One day she said, "I must have something to eat."

So she went to get some corn. When she came back she found something big and white in her nest.

"Dear me, what is that?" she said. And away she ran to tell Black Hen.

"Good day," said Black Hen to White Hen.

But White Hen did not say, "Good day." She could not stop for that. She said:

"Oh, Black Hen, something white is in my nest."

"Did you look at it?" asked Black Hen.

"I did," said White Hen. "Then I ran over here to tell you."

"Let us go and tell Brown Duck about it. I will call my sister Clucker and my brother Top-knot and they can go, too."

So White Hen, Black Hen, her sister Clucker,

61

and her brother Top-knot went to tell Brown Duck about it.

Brown Duck saw them coming. She said, "Good day, White Hen."

White Hen could not stop to say, "Good day." She said, "Something white is in my nest."

Then Black Hen, her sister Clucker, and her brother Top-knot said, "Yes, something white is in her nest."

"Did you look at it?" said Brown Duck.

"I did," said White Hen.

And Black Hen, her sister Clucker, and her brother Top-knot said, "She did."

"I will call my three big brother ducks. We will all go and see Wise Owl. He will tell us how to find out what it is."

So Brown Duck and her three big brother ducks, Black Hen, her sister Clucker, her brother Top-knot, all went with White Hen to call on Wise Owl.

The owl's house was in a big tree back of the barn. Wise Owl saw them coming. He said, "Good day, White Hen."

White Hen could not stop to say, "Good day." She

said, "Oh, Wise Owl, something big and white is in my nest."

Then Black Hen, her sister Clucker, her brother Top-knot, Brown Duck and her three big brother ducks, all said:

"Yes, something big and white is in her nest."

"Did you look at it?" asked Wise Owl.

"I did," said White Hen.

And Black Hen, her sister Clucker, her brother Top-knot, Brown Duck and her three big brother ducks, all said:

"She did."

Then Wise Owl said, "Let me think."   Then he said, "We must go into the barn.   We must find out what is in White Hen's nest."

So Black Hen, her sister Clucker, her brother Top-knot, Brown Duck and her three big brother ducks, and Wise Owl all went with White Hen to the barn.

When they got there Wise Owl said, "Stand back, I will call.   Who!   Who!   Who is in White Hen's nest?"

What do you think they saw in the nest?   A white kitty!

And a little one at that!

"Dear me," said White Hen, "I wish I had looked carefully. I know that kitty."

And Black Hen, her sister Clucker, her brother Topknot, Brown Duck and her three big brother ducks, and Wise Owl said: "She knows that kitty."

And Wise Owl said:

> "It's just a kitty,
> What a pity!"

JOLLY MR. WIND

"I don't like the wind!" cried Betty, as she lay in her little bed, waiting for her nap to come along, while she listened to the wind "woohing" about the house.

"You don't!" said a weeny voice that sounded so like a chime of bells that Betty sat right up in bed, to see a dear little Butterfly Fairy teetering on the brass bedpost.

"No," she repeated, "I don't like it. It rattles the windows and makes the trees squeak. I wish it would never blow. I don't see what it's good for!"

"Dear me!" cried the Fairy. "Come!" And in a moment Betty found she too was a Butterfly Fairy with silvery wings, floating far away.

"See that boy crying?" asked the Fairy. "His kite won't fly. You didn't like the wind and it stopped blowing."

"It's a beautiful kite," said Betty. "Looks like a bird."

"Yes, his uncle sent it from Japan."

"I wish the wind would blow. I'd like to see it fly."

"You would?" asked the fairy.   "Then watch."

The Fairy wand swept the air, the wind began to blow, the bird kite spread its wings and soared higher and higher, while the boy shouted with joyous laughter.

"It's a lovely game," said Betty.   "Show me some more things the wind can do."

Betty and the Fairy floated on, and presently paused above a group of children gazing sadly at some wee boats lazily rocking at the edge of a stream.

"How unhappy they look," said Betty.

"Yes, they are very poor and have few toys.   Their father carved them each a little boat; the mother made the sails. To-day they were to celebrate a birthday by sailing them, but a certain little girl didn't like the wind, and it stopped blowing."

"Oh! make it blow.   I'd love to see the boats sail!" cried Betty, and in a moment the wind began to whistle its merry tune, the sails filled, and the boats glided along so fast that the boys had to run while they held tight to the strings lest the boats sail far from shore.

"Don't they look pretty!" cried Betty.   "Just like sea gulls."

"Indeed they do; but we must be off."

As they floated above a certain village, Betty exclaimed, "Oh! how untidy it is."

"Yes, because you didn't want the wind to blow. The wind has a fine broom and tidies up the world as nothing else can."

"Let it sweep the streets. I'd love to see it," said Betty.

"The wind is a cheery body. It always sings as it works," said the Fairy, and they listened to its song while it swished its great broom about, sweeping the dust and papers in a swirling mass far away, leaving the village streets as clean as a whistle.

"Isn't it lovely!" cried Betty, clapping her hands. "I didn't know it could really sweep."

"There is no end to the things it can do. Come over here where you can see that line full of soggy wet clothes. If the wind could blow for a while they would quickly dry, and that little mother could take them in and sprinkle them ready for to-morrow's ironing. If it doesn't blow, her work will go wrong all the week, and then she just can't take the children to the circus Saturday."

"Let it blow!" cried Betty, and in a moment the clothes

were gayly flapping in the breeze, while Betty watched, amazed to see how fast they were drying.

"See that flag!" she said presently as they sped onward. "Doesn't it look beautiful fluttering so gayly."

"Of course, but it's the wind that tosses its colors about; and see the clouds, they look like a flock of sheep tumbling around on the blue sky; and do you see that splendid gold rooster on that barn? You can almost hear him crying, 'Cockadoodledoo, the wind and I show you when to plant your grain and what to do to-day because to-morrow it will rain!' It is most important for the farmers to know what the weather is to be, and the wind tells them as the rooster rides on his merry-go-round. In Holland almost everything is done by the windmills. If the wind didn't blow Holland would be sad indeed."

"I wish I could see the wind," said Betty. "He is so splendid."

"That's one reason why he is so splendid, because you can't see him. I want to show you one more beautiful thing the wind can do. It can play exquisite music, the sweetest you can imagine. Come."

Wonderingly Betty followed, to see presently a dear

little boy sitting on a porch near a window in which was placed an æolian harp. The child sat patiently waiting, with such a wistful little face that Betty asked, "Why is he so sad?"

"He cannot see the beautiful world. Some one gave him this harp, but it cannot play unless the wind blows. Listen!"

"I don't wonder that he wanted to hear it," said Betty. "I never heard such beautiful music!"

They listened for a while to the harmony breathed forth from the wind-swept strings. Then Betty found the music had done its work; the boy was asleep with such a smile of peace and joy that she whispered gently: "I love the wind. I hope it will always blow. I love to feel it kissing my cheeks, and I am so glad I know about it."

"Of course you are. He is one of the busiest of Mother Nature's children—a jolly, rollicking fellow, and we just couldn't get along without him."

As the Fairy talked they were floating toward home, and soon Betty found herself snuggled in her little bed listening to the "woohing" sounds.

"It 'ha ha ha's' every time it does one of those splendid

things, and now it's singing me to sleep," she murmured as the drowsy eyes closed and the wind song grew more and more gentle and finally died away.

THE LITTLE ROUND RED APPLE

A little girl saw a round red apple in a tree. It hung on a branch just over her head. She tried to get it. She jumped and jumped and jumped. But she could not reach it.

Then she said, "O please, round red apple, come down to me." But the apple did not drop down.

A little bird flew into the tree. He rested on a branch near the round red apple.

Then the little girl said, "O please, little bird, sing to the round red apple and make it come down to me."

The little bird sang and sang, but the round red apple did not drop down.

The little girl said, "I'll ask the sun to help me. Please, sun, shine on the round red apple and make it drop down to me."

The sun shone and shone. But the round red apple did not drop down.

Soon the wind came blustering by.

The little girl said, "O blustering wind, help me to get that round red apple."

"Woo-oo-oo," blew the blustering wind. "Woo-oo-oo." He shook the tree and it bent this way and that way. Then plump! Down fell the red apple into the little girl's lap.

"Thank you, blustering wind," she said.

WHO LIKES NUTS?

"Mamma, do dogs like nuts?" asked Bobby one winter morning as he came hurrying in from the yard.

"No, Bobby. Why do you ask?"

"I left a good many on the bench in the yard last night, and they are all gone this morning. Perhaps kitty took them."

"Oh, no," said mamma, "kitties don't like nuts. It must have been some visitor to our yard. Come, let us see."

Bobby followed his mamma and showed her where he had left the nuts the night before. Yes, they were all gone and neither Bobby nor his mamma could tell what had become of them. Jip stood by wagging his tail and wondering what it all meant.

"Never mind, Bobby; perhaps the little visitor will remember his feast and come again soon. Then we can see who he is."

"Now, Jip," whispered Bobby, "you must watch. If you

see any strange creature come into our yard, bark and bark. I'll watch from the window. The snow is too deep for me to play out here with you any longer."

Then Bobby went into the house. He was quite faithful to his watch for a little while, but it was tiresome work for a little boy. And wasn't Jip in the yard to let him know if anything should happen? So when Bobby left the window he would soon have forgotten all about the nuts and Jip, too, if a sharp bark in the yard had not told him that something was wrong. Bobby hurried to the window but he could see nothing. Jip was still barking and there were a number of tiny tracks around the doorstep, but nothing else that Bobby could see. Oh, how Jip did wish to tell Bobby something. But it was time for Jip to have his dinner and the poor little fellow was hungry after his long watch.

Some one else was quite hungry, too, and Jip knew who it was. Yes, he had seen Gray Squirrel peep his head out of the hollow at the top of the tree, and creep quietly down in search of a dinner. How Jip did wish to tell Bobby!

There was no dog in the yard now and the thought of

the last feast of nuts made Gray Squirrel very brave once more.

Quietly he crept down from his home in the tree. He made no sound but he left some tiny tracks that told the whole story to Bobby and Jip. Soon Gray Squirrel reached the bench. It was the place where he had found such good nuts only the night before. But alas! no nuts were there now; and nothing else, not even a bite for Gray Squirrel.

"Perhaps I can find something near the house," he thought.

No doubt Gray Squirrel would have found a good breakfast near the doorstep if some one had not opened the door just at that moment.

"Oh, mamma, see the little squirrel. There! He has just scampered up the tree. Do you think he is the one who took my nuts?"

Then mamma told Bobby how dearly the squirrels love nuts. "No doubt this was the little visitor who came last night. Perhaps he has the nuts stored away somewhere for his food during the winter."

"Can you see him now, mamma?"

"No, but I think his home must be in the hollow of that old tree where the birds stayed last summer."

"Do you think he will stay there all winter?"

"We'll help him to get his dinners and breakfasts and then he will not need to find another home until the birds come back."

"What a nice visitor he will be every morning!" said Bobby.

Gray Squirrel often found some nuts on the bench when he went to hunt for his breakfast. Do *you* think he stayed the rest of the winter?

HOW LAZY-BONES WAS CURED

Watch Barker was his real name, but no one ever called him that. He couldn't keep awake long enough to watch and it was too much work to bark. He was the laziest dog you ever saw.

One day his mother sent him for some meat. He fell asleep on the way and Sly Hound stole the meat.

She sent him for some milk and he was so long coming back that it turned sour.

She wanted some clean straw for a bed for the babies, but he forgot and went to sleep on it himself. If he started to chase a kitten he would give up before the kitten knew she was being chased.

All he wanted to do was to sleep and eat. And he wouldn't even bother to get his food, but would howl if it was not brought to him.

Do you wonder that they called him "Lazy-Bones"?

The farm people said they had never seen such a dog in all their lives, and that something must be done.

Rooster Strut called a meeting to talk it over.

"I know a way to cure him," said Goat Graybeard. "And we'll keep at him till it does."

And then they had a secret meeting.

The next morning the sun saw a strange procession marching from the barn.

First came Horse Faithful, then Cow Gentle, then Goat Graybeard, then Pig Greedy, then Mother Barker, Cat Mouser, Turkey Thanks, Goose Gander, Duck Paddler, Rooster Strut, Hen Scratcher, and last of all Chicken Peep.

Slowly they marched to Mother Barker's house.   In a row they stood before it.   Ready!   Now!

"Neigh! neigh!" said Horse Faithful.

"Moo! moo!" said Cow Gentle.

"Baa! Baa!" said Goat Graybeard.

"Bow-wow!" said Mother Barker.

"Meow! Meow!" said Cat Mouser.

"Gobble! Gobble!" said Turkey Thanks.

"Honk! Honk!" said Goose Gander.

"Quack! Quack!" said Duck Paddle.

"Cock-a-doodle-doo!" said Rooster Strut.

They carried the basket of apples home.

Page 54

The little girl said, "I'll ask the sun to help me."

Page 71

"Cluck! Cluck!" said Hen Scratcher.

"Peep! Peep!" said Chicken Peep.

Lazy-Bones sprang up, rushed out of the kennel and set up a howl.

"Will you stay awake all day?" asked the Horse, the Cat, the Goat, the Pig, the Dog, the Cow, the Turkey, the Goose, the Duck, the Rooster, the Hen, and the Chicken all together.

"Oh! I will, I will," whined Lazy-Bones.

And he did; for if he gave even a wink they would all set up the din again.

The next day Horse Faithful thought he didn't need to help, and the next day Cow Gentle saw she needn't. The day after Goat Graybeard dropped out and the next Pig Greedy. Then Mother Barker didn't bark, and Cat Mouser didn't meow. Only Turkey Thanks and Goose Gander and Duck Paddler, Rooster Strut, Hen Scratcher and Chicken Peep were left. And one by one each day they stopped till only Chicken Peep was left on duty.

And it would take only the tiniest little peep from him to make Lazy-Bones wide awake.

Oh, I forgot, we mustn't call him Lazy-Bones any

longer, for the other day Mother Barker sent him for meat and he brought it straight home. She sent him for milk and it came sweet. She wanted straw and the babies had it in five minutes.

He always gets his own food now and yesterday he really chased a kitten.

Reprinted by permission from "The Story Hour."

THE BACK YARD PARTY

Mrs. Mouse had been hard at work all the morning. She had asked her friends to a garden party in her back yard.

The field mice were to be there. She had also asked the mice at the barn, and of course the house mice were to come, too.

At first the house mice thought they would not go. They had always felt themselves a little better than the others. But when they heard that there was to be a dance, nothing could keep the young mice away. And the old mice knew they must go to look after the young ones.

Mrs. Mouse was very happy when she learned that all her friends were coming. When the night of the party came she said to her children:

"You may sit up late to see the fun. But you must promise first to be very good."

"We promise to be *very* good, mother dear," they all said.

They stood up in a row with their paws folded, and very funny indeed, they looked.

The first to come were the mice at the barn. They lived very near.

By the time the moon was shining bright and clear all were there.

And such a good time as they had! Old and young danced and danced in the light of the moon.

When they grew tired of the dance one merry young mouse called out, "Let's play leap-frog!"

"Yes, yes," the others shouted. "Leap-frog! We'll all play leap-frog."

They all stood in a row waiting for the word to start.

The leader called out, "One! Two! Three!" But before she could say, "Go!" the house door opened. The players turned to see who was coming. Out ran the big gray cat.

"I smell a mouse," they heard her say.

They did not wait to hear any more. As quick as a wink, Mrs. Mouse's garden party was over. Not one mouse waited to say, "Good-by." Not one even took the trouble to tell Mrs. Mouse what a good time he had had.

THE DISCONTENTED PIG

There was once a little curly-tailed pig that lived by himself. His house was at the edge of the village.

Every day he worked in his garden. Whether the sun shone or the rain fell, he dug and hoed and weeded his garden. He turned the earth around his tomato vines. He loosened the soil of his carrot bed. In time he had the finest vegetables in the kingdom. People heard about them and they traveled from many countries to see his garden.

One day this little pig said, "It is hard to work in a garden day after day. I shall go out in the world and find an easier way to earn a living."

So he shut the door of his house, turned the lock, and put the key into his pocket. Then away he went.

He had traveled several miles when he came to a little cottage. As he drew near he heard lovely music.

Now it happened that a cat lived in that snug cottage. He earned his living by playing the fiddle. Little Pig saw the cat standing in the door. It was he who was making the sweet sounds.

"Surely that is an easy way of earning a living. And it must be much pleasanter than digging in a garden! Will you teach me to play the fiddle, Friend Cat?" he asked.

"Certainly," said the cat.

He gave Little Pig the bow and the fiddle. Little Pig took them and began to pull the bow across the fiddle. Squeak! Quang! Oh, what a sound!

"This isn't music," said Little Pig.

"It certainly is not," said the cat. "You haven't tried long enough. If you wish to play the fiddle you must work!"

"Then I'll look for something else," said Little Pig. "This is quite as hard as weeding a garden."

He gave back the bow and the fiddle to the cat and started down the road.

On and on he went until he came to a hut. In the hut lived a dog who made cheese. Little Pig saw him making the curd into cakes.

"That looks quite easy," said Little Pig. "I'd like to make cheese myself."

So he asked the dog to teach him. This the dog was willing to do. Soon Little Pig was at work beside the dog. As he worked he grew hot and tired. Then he stopped to rest and fan himself.

"No, no, don't do that," said the dog. "You will spoil the cheese. There can be no rest till the work is done."

"Oh dear," said Little Pig. "This is as hard as growing vegetables or playing the fiddle. I must look for something easier."

And he started down the road.

On the side of the river Little Pig saw a man taking honey out of beehives. The hives were in a sweet green field. Little Pig thought that that was the work which he would like best.

"It must be lovely there in the meadow among the flowers. Honey is not heavy to lift, and once in a while I can eat some."

He ran to the man as fast as he could go. "I should like to work with bees," said Little Pig.

This plan pleased the bee man as much as it pleased Little Pig.

"Begin at once," said the man.

He gave Little Pig a veil. Also, he gave him a pair of gloves.

"Fasten these on well," said the man. "Then lift the honeycomb out of the hive."

Little Pig ran to do so. How happy he was! But buzz buzz buzz! The bees crept under his veil and inside his gloves. They stung him on his feet, his mouth, his ears, and the end of his nose.

Did you ever hear a little pig squeal? How that little pig squealed. And he ran, too.

"Come back!" called the man.

"No, no," squealed Little Pig. "The bees hurt me."

"Of course they do," said the man. "They hurt me, too! That is part of the work. You cannot work with bees without getting stung."

Then Little Pig blinked his eyes and began to think hard.

"Every kind of work has something hard about it. It made my arms ache to play the fiddle. When I made cheese I couldn't stop a minute until it was done. In taking honey from the hive the bees sting you till your head is on fire. Work in my garden is not so bad. I'm going back to it."

And he went.

THE TALE OF PETER RABBIT

Once upon a time there were four little rabbits, and their names were—   Flopsy,

Mopsy,

Cotton-tail,

and Peter.

They lived with their mother in a sand-bank underneath the root of a very big fir tree.

"Now, my dears," said old Mrs. Rabbit, one morning, "you may go into the fields or down the lane.   But don't go into Mr. McGregor's garden.   Your father had an accident there; he was put in a pie by Mrs. McGregor. Now run along, and don't get into mischief.   I am going out."

Then old Mrs. Rabbit took a basket and her umbrella, and went through the wood to the baker's.   She bought a loaf of brown bread and five currant buns.

Flopsy, Mopsy, and Cotton-tail, who were good little bunnies, went down the lane to gather blackberries, but

Peter, who was naughty, ran straight away to Mr. Mc-Gregor's garden, and squeezed under the gate!

First he ate some lettuce and some beans. Then he ate some radishes. Then feeling rather sick, he went to look for some parsley.

But round the end of a cucumber frame, whom should he meet but Mr. McGregor!

Mr. McGregor was on his hands and knees planting out young cabbages, but he jumped up and ran after Peter, waving a rake and calling out, "Stop, thief!"

Peter was dreadfully frightened. He rushed all over the garden, for he had forgotten the way back to the gate.

He lost one of his shoes among the cabbages and the other shoe among the potatoes.

After losing them he ran on four legs, and went faster, so that I think he might have got away altogether if he had not unfortunately run into a gooseberry net, and was caught by the large buttons on his jacket. It was a blue jacket with brass buttons, quite new.

Peter gave himself up for lost, and shed big tears; but his sobs were overheard by some friendly sparrows, who flew to him in great excitement, and implored him to exert himself.

Mr. McGregor came up with a sieve, which he intended to pop upon the top of Peter; but Peter wriggled out just in time, leaving his jacket behind him, and rushed into the tool-shed, and jumped into a can. It would have been a beautiful thing to hide in, if it had not had so much water in it.

Mr. McGregor was quite sure that Peter was somewhere in the tool-shed, perhaps hidden underneath a flower-pot. He began to turn them over carefully, looking under each.

Presently Peter sneezed—"Kerchoo!" Mr. McGregor was after him in no time, and tried to put his foot upon Peter, who jumped out of a window, upsetting three plants. The window was too small for Mr. McGregor, and he was tired of running after Peter. He went back to his work.

Peter sat down to rest; he was out of breath and trembling with fright, and he had not the least idea which way to go.

Also, he was very damp from sitting in that can.

After a time he began to wander about, going—lippity-lippity—not very fast, and looking all around.

He found a door in a wall; but it was locked, and there was no room for a fat little rabbit to squeeze underneath.

An old mouse was running in and out over the stone doorstep, carrying peas and beans to her family in the wood. Peter asked her the way to the gate, but she had such a large pea in her mouth that she could not answer. She only shook her head at him. Peter began to cry.

Then he tried to find his way straight across the garden, but he became more and more puzzled. Presently he came to a pond where Mr. McGregor filled his water-cans.

A white cat was staring at some goldfish; she sat very, very still, but now and then the tip of her tail twitched as if it were alive.

Peter thought it best to go away without speaking to her; he had heard about cats from his cousin, Benjamin Bunny.

He went back towards the tool-shed, but suddenly, quite close to him, he heard a noise of a hoe—scr-r-ritch, scratch, scratch, scritch. Peter scuttled underneath the bushes.

But presently, as nothing happened, he came out, and climbed upon a wheelbarrow and peeped over. The first thing he saw was Mr. McGregor hoeing onions.   His back was towards Peter, and beyond him was the gate!

Peter got down very quietly off the wheelbarrow, and started running as fast as he could go, along a straight walk behind some black-currant bushes.

Mr. McGregor caught sight of him at the corner, but Peter did not care.   He slipped underneath the gate, and was safe at last in the wood outside the garden.

Mr. McGregor hung up the little jacket and the shoes for a scare-crow to frighten the blackbirds.

Peter was so tired that he flopped down upon the soft sand on the floor of the rabbit-hole, and shut his eyes.

His mother was busy cooking; she wondered what he had done with his clothes.   It was the second little jacket and pair of shoes that Peter had lost in a fortnight.

I am sorry to say that Peter was not very well during the evening.

His mother put him to bed, and made some camomile tea; and she gave a dose of it to Peter!   "One tablespoonful to be taken at bed-time."

But Flopsy, Mopsy, and Cotton-tail had bread and milk and blackberries for supper.

TWO LITTLE SUNBEAMS

"Hickamore, Hackamore,
  On the King's kitchen door.
  All the King's horses, and all the King's men
  Could not get Hickamore, Hackamore
  Off the King's kitchen door."

Old Rhyme

There was once upon a time a very gloomy King, who lived in a very gloomy castle. The castle had thick walls, and small windows that were never opened. On three sides were great forests of pine trees that grew close up to the building, even up to the front door. On the fourth side there was only a low hedge. From the kitchen door stretched a wide avenue which led to the nearest city.

The king never went to the kitchen door, and hardly knew of the wide avenue, or of the city. He sat all day looking out at the dark, gloomy pine trees in front of his castle. He was always lonely and always sad. All his

93

servants also had rooms in the front of the castle. And they were as gloomy as the king himself.

The one merry person in the castle was the kitchen-maid. She did her work by the open kitchen door, and she often went down the avenue to the city to hear the news.

One fine April morning two dancing little strangers, dressed in bright yellow, came running up the avenue from the city to the king's castle. Instead of going to the front door, as strangers usually did, they came bouncing along to the open kitchen door. One jumped upon the door knocker, the other upon the door handle. Then both began kicking at the door with all their might.

"Who are you?" called out the kitchen-maid. She was cleaning the boots in the doorway. "And what do you want?"

"I'm Hickamore," said one, standing on his head on the door handle.

"I'm Hackamore," said the other, turning a somersault through the knocker.

"We want to see the king," they said.

And then they began to run up and down the door with

all their might. The kitchen-maid did not seem at all surprised at this.

She began to laugh merrily, and said, "Well, you won't see the king if you stay there. You will have to go round to the front door."

"But we are *not* going round to the front door. We are going to stay where we are. And we must see the king."

They ran up and down the kitchen door faster than before, now here, now there. They were two bright spots of color against the brown wood.

At this the little kitchen-maid laughed so merrily and loud that the head cook, who was busy cooking the king's favorite dish, looked up and exclaimed, "What's the matter?"

"Oh," said the kitchen-maid, as well as she could for laughing, "it's Hickamore and Hackamore. They are on the king's kitchen door, and they wish to see the king."

"Then why don't they go round to the front door?" asked the head cook.

"They don't want to," said the kitchen-maid.

The head cook was so surprised that, spoon in hand,

he came out into the passage to see the two strangers. They were still running up and down the kitchen door as fast as ever they could. As soon as the head cook set eyes on them he burst out laughing.

"Good gracious me!" he called out. And raising the big wooden spoon he was carrying he waved it in the air.

At this moment a page-boy arrived at the other end of the passage. He was coming into the kitchen to fetch the king's pudding. He was a gloomy youth, with straight hair. When he saw the head cook at the kitchen door, waving his spoon in the air and laughing he stopped still.

With his mouth wide open, he called out, "What's the matter?"

"It's Hickamore and Hackamore," said the head cook, still waving his spoon in the air. "They are on the king's kitchen door, and they want to see the king."

"Why don't they go round to the front door then?" asked the page-boy, coming forward.

"They don't want to," said the head cook.

By this time the page-boy had also come to the kitchen door. Hickamore and Hackamore were still running up and down with all their might. As soon as the page-boy set eyes on them *he* began to roar with laughter, and his straight hair began to curl.

"Well, I never!" said he.

All this time the king was waiting for his favorite dish. A lady-in-waiting was sent down to the kitchen to tell the page-boy to hurry. She was a very gloomy lady with stiff starched petticoats and very stiff knees. As she came into the passage she saw the page-boy standing at the kitchen door laughing and laughing. His hair was now curling all over his head!

"Whatever *is* the matter?" said she, very stiffly.

"Oh, dear me! It is Hickamore and Hackamore!" said the page-boy. "They are on the king's kitchen door, and they want to see the king."

"Why do they not go round to the front door then?" said the lady-in-waiting still more stiffly.

"They don't want to," laughed the page-boy.

The lady-in-waiting walked slowly down the passage to see the two queer strangers. Hickamore and Hackamore had never stopped running up and down the kitchen door as fast as ever they could go.

No sooner had the lady-in-waiting set eyes on them than *she* began to laugh. All the stiffness went out of her petticoats and out of her knees. She took the page-boy around the waist and danced with him all the way up the passage. At the end of it they bumped into the Lord High Chamberlain, who had come down to see why the king had not received his favorite pudding.

"I beg your pardon," said the lady-in-waiting, but she did not stop laughing.

"What *is* the matter?" said the Lord High Chamberlain, who was a terribly gloomy person, almost as gloomy as the king himself.

"If you please," said the lady-in-waiting, "it is Hickamore and Hackamore. They are on the king's door, and they want to see the king."

"Let them be shown round to the front door then!" said the Lord High Chamberlain.

"But they don't want to," said the lady-in-waiting.

"They will *have* to want to," answered the Lord High Chamberlain, as he went down the passage to the kitchen door.

By this time Hickamore was standing on his head on

the door handle, and Hackamore was turning somersaults very fast through the knocker. For one whole minute the Lord High Chamberlain stared at them. Then, very slowly a smile appeared on his face. The smile grew broader and broader, and then, "Ha! Ha! Ha!" laughed he.

Then he gathered up his robes and skipped—yes he *skipped* along the passage, and upstairs to see the king. He was followed by the lady-in-waiting, the page-boy, and the head cook. The kitchen-maid stayed where she was and went on cleaning the boots, and Hickamore and Hackamore were running up and down the kitchen door again just as if nothing had happened.

All this time the king had been waiting in the banqueting-hall for his favorite dish. This room was very long, very low, and very dark. The pine trees pressed close up against the windows, which were shut. His majesty sat at the end of the long banqueting table with his head bowed down. Many servants, all very gloomy and stiff, stood around him, but they kept their eyes fixed on the ground. No one spoke a word.

Suddenly, the door at the other end of the room burst

open.   In skipped the Lord High Chamberlain and behind him danced the lady-in-waiting.   Her petticoats were soft and clinging.   Behind her danced the page-boy and his hair now curled all over his head!   Behind him leaped the head cook waving his wooden spoon in the air!

The king looked up at them without a smile on his face.   In a moment the Lord High Chamberlain dropped into a walk.   The lady-in-waiting seemed to feel her knees growing stiff again.   The page-boy's hair began to uncurl and the head cook dropped his spoon with a clatter.

"Where is my favorite dish?" said the king wearily.

The head cook fled.   So did the page-boy.   So did the lady-in-waiting, shutting the door after her.   The Lord High Chamberlain stood alone in the middle of the floor. Nobody spoke a word.

"Well?" said the king at last.

"Please, your Majesty," began the Lord High Chamberlain, "it is Hickamore and Hackamore.   They are on your kitchen door, and they want to see you."

"Let them come round to the front door then."

"They don't want to."

There was another long silence.

"Send all my horses and all my men to fetch them!"
The Lord High Chamberlain bowed and left the room.

Soon the page-boy appeared, carrying the king's favorite
dish. His hair was quite straight again. The lady-in-
waiting followed him, and her knees were as stiff as ever;
but there was just a hint of laughter in her eyes.

All this time the little kitchen-maid was busy cleaning
the boots, and Hickamore and Hackamore were still running up and down the kitchen door as fast as ever they
could go.

Presently, along the avenue came the tramp, tramp,
tramp of horses' hoofs. Two and two they came—all the
king's horses and all the king's men! The leader rode
in front on a beautiful white horse.

Hickamore and Hackamore paid no attention to any
of them, but began a game of "Catch" up and down the
kitchen door.

All the king's horses and all the king's men came nearer
and nearer. At last they drew up in two long lines just
opposite the kitchen door. A herald blew a long blast
upon his trumpet. The leader went to the kitchen door
and saluted.

"We have come to take you to the front door," said he to Hickamore and Hackamore. Then all of a sudden, he began to laugh and laugh and his white horse under him started prancing.

Hickamore and Hackamore stopped their game of "Catch." They sat quite still side by side on the knocker, winking at the leader. He raised his hand. This was the signal for arrest in that country.

Four of the king's horses and four of the king's men came to arrest Hickamore and Hackamore, but as soon as they set eyes upon the two little strangers they began to laugh, and the horses grew so unmanageable that they could not get anywhere near the door!

Hickamore and Hackamore were still winking at the leader. He held up his hand again, and another four horses and men came forward to try their luck. But as soon as they set eyes upon the two little strangers they began to laugh.

And so it went on until every horse and man had tried to get Hickamore and Hackamore off the king's kitchen door. And not one could. There the two queer little creatures sat on the knocker, winking at each new-comer.

Then the men tried to get off their horses and catch Hickamore and Hackamore on foot, but the horses all seemed bewitched, and the men found it quite impossible.

The Lord High Chamberlain, who had been watching them from a top window, gave a signal to the leader. All the king's horses and all the king's men went tramp! tramp! tramp! the way they had come.

The kitchen-maid went on with her boots again laughing more merrily than before. Hickamore and Hackamore started to run up the kitchen door just as if nothing had happened.

The Lord High Chamberlain went once more to the king.

"Your Majesty," said he, "it is of no use. All your horses and all your men can not get them off the kitchen door!"

"Who saw them first?" asked the king.

"The kitchen-maid," said the Lord High Chamberlain.

"Bring her here!" said the king.

In a few minutes the little kitchen-maid was brought before the king. She was rosy and fresh and she was still laughing.

"Who are these strangers?" asked the king.

"They are only two little sunbeams! your Majesty," said the kitchen-maid.

The king stared.

"How can I bring them in here?" he asked.

"Cut down the pine trees all around the castle, open the windows, and you will see them in a twinkling," said she.

"Thank you," said the king.

Then turning to the Lord High Chamberlain and speaking in a loud, clear voice he said, "Cut down the pine trees all round the castle, and open the windows!"

The Lord High Chamberlain bowed and left the room.

Then began such hewing and sawing and splitting as never had been heard in all that country-side! Every one from the city, indeed, every one from the kingdom came to help. The pages and courtiers and ladies-in-waiting went to open the windows, and very stiff they found them.

At last every tree was down, and every window opened. The sun streamed into the castle. The king rose from his throne like a man waking out of a dream. All the people followed him. The exercise of opening the windows had made every one much less stiff and gloomy

than before. The king went slowly down to the front door.
He opened it. In bounced Hickamore and Hackamore,
one after the other!

"We have come in to see you at last!" cried they, and
danced about his crown.

The door stood wide open. As the king looked out he
thought he could see many other little Hickamores and
Hackamores at merry games on the grass. Then he threw
back his head and laughed.

"Ha! Ha! Ha! Let us join them," said he.

Out on to the lawn he danced, with all his people after
him. Never was seen such a merry party. Among them
all, here, there, and everywhere, danced Hickamore and
Hackamore. For the little kitchen-maid was quite right.
They were only two little sunbeams!

WHAT THEY DO

"I shine," says the Sun,
"To give the world light."
"I glimmer," adds the Moon,
"To beautify the night."
"I ripple," says the Brook.
"I whisper," sighs the Breeze.
"I patter," laughs the Rain.
"We rustle," call the Trees.
"We dance," nod the Daisies.
"I twinkle," shines the Star.
"We sing," chant the Birds,
"How happy we all are!"
"I smile," cries the child,
Gentle, good, and gay;
The sweetest thing of all,
The sunshine of each day.

GRANDMOTHER'S
NURSERY CORNER

HOW BUTTERFLIES CAME

One day the flowers begged the fairies to let them leave their stalks and fly away into the air.

"We have to sit here in the same place from morning till night, fairies! Do let us go!"

"Go then, dear flowers," said the fairies. "But you must promise that you will return to your stalks before the sun goes down."

"We promise," called out the flowers, red, yellow, and white, as they flew away, over the grass, out of the garden, to the great wide meadow beyond. The fairies' garden seemed suddenly to have taken wings.

As the sun rose the next morning there was a flutter of stalks, and when the fairies came they found each flower again in its place.

"Well done, well done!" exclaimed the fairies. "To-morrow you may fly away again to the meadows."

As the sun rose the next morning there was a flutter of red and yellow and white, as, from every stalk, a pair of colored wings rose and flapped, then took flight once more over the meadows and fields. And by and by a day came when the petals of the flowers became wings—*real* wings, for the flowers themselves had become beautiful butter-flies—red, yellow, and white.

WHO WOKE LITTLE BOY BLUE?

Mother Hen and her little chicks loved to play in the meadow where the red clover grew. Mother Hen was very wise. She always took a peep under the gate to make sure that all was safe. If she said, "Cluck, Cluck," away ran the little chicks to have a scratch among the sweet clover blooms.

One bright sunny morning they came to the gate and Mother Hen took a peep under it, as usual. "Dear me," she cried as she lifted her head and looked all around.

"What is it, mother?" peeped all the little chicks.

"Dear me, dear me! Something dreadful has happened. We must not go into the meadow."

"I want to run and hide in the clover," peeped one little chick.

"And I'd like to hunt little stones and bugs," called out another.

"Cluck, cluck, cluck! We must not go in, I say. The

sheep is in the meadow and the cow is in the corn! It is not safe for my chicks."

"Where shall we go, mother?" peeped all the little chicks.

"You must run back to the barnyard, while I try to find the little boy who looks after the sheep."

Away ran the little chicks. Away ran Mother Hen to find Little Boy Blue. She did not know which way to go, so she ran this way and that way as Mother Hens do.

Mrs. Gray Squirrel, who was peeping out of her hole in the tree, saw Mother Hen.

"Good morning, Mother Hen," she called out. "Where are you running so early?"

"Oh, Mrs. Gray Squirrel, such a dreadful thing has happened. The sheep is in the meadow and the cow is in the corn. It is not safe for my chicks to go there. Can you tell me where to find Little Boy Blue? He looks after the sheep, you know."

"You say the sheep is in the meadow and the cow is in the corn? Then it is not safe for my baby squirrels to frisk in the clover. I will go with you to find Little Boy Blue. He must look after his sheep."

Mother Hen did not wait to hear what Mrs. Gray Squirrel said to her little ones, but she ran on and on. Soon she came to the barnyard and in a little while Mrs. Gray Squirrel stood beside her.

There they found Dame Duck getting her ducklings ready for a good swim in the pond beyond the meadow.

"Oh, Dame Duck," cried Mother Hen, "a dreadful thing has happened. The sheep is in the meadow and the cow is in the corn. The meadow is not a safe place for my chicks. Can you tell me where to find the little boy who looks after the sheep?"

"Indeed, I cannot, Mother Hen. But these ducklings of mine must not go to the pond to swim. It is not safe for them even to walk through the meadow. Ducklings must stay in the barnyard. I will go with you to find Little Boy Blue."

Away ran Mother Hen, Mrs. Gray Squirrel, and Dame Duck.

"Umph! Umph!" called out Mother Pig from her corner in the sty. "What is all this fuss about?"

"Oh, Mother Pig, the sheep is in the meadow and the

cow is in the corn. It is not safe for my chicks to run and scratch in the clover."

"Nor for my squirrels to run and frisk about," said Mrs. Gray Squirrel.

"Nor for my ducklings to go to the duck-pond," quacked Dame Duck.

"Umph! Then my little pigs must stay in the sty. They can't have a roll on the mud-bank. What are you going to do about it?"

"We are trying to find the little boy who looks after the sheep. Can you tell us where he is?"

"I haven't the least idea. But I'll go with you, if it isn't far."

"Cheer-up, cheer-up," called Robin Redbreast as he watched Gray Squirrel, Dame Duck, and Mother Pig follow Mother Hen wherever she led them.

"Oh, Robin Redbreast," called out Mother Hen as she caught sight of his red breast among the branches of a tree overhead. "Do help us to find Little Boy Blue."

"Little Boy Blue is over there under the haystack. I stood on the haystack and sang him a little song this morning. I'll lead you to him. Watch where I fly."

Away flew Robin Redbreast and away ran Mother Hen and the others. They soon reached the haystack; and there, under the haystack was Little Boy Blue fast asleep.

"Cluck, cluck, cluck!" called out Mother Hen as soon as she saw him. "He's fast asleep. My cluck, cluck does not wake him. Will you try, Gray Squirrel?"

"Oh, no, not I, for if I do, he'll be sure to cry."

"Will you wake him, Dame Duck?"

"Oh, no, not I, for if I do, he'll be sure to cry."

"Mother Pig, you'll wake Little Boy Blue, won't you?"

"Oh, no, not I, for if I do, he'll be sure to cry."

"Dear me, dear me, what can I do? We must wake up Little Boy Blue."

"What is all the noise about?" asked Red Cock as he came to join the others.

"Oh, Red Cock," said Mother Hen, "I can't wake up Little Boy Blue. The sheep is in the meadow and the cow is in the corn. I asked Gray Squirrel and Dame Duck and Mother Pig to wake him but they all said:

" 'Oh, no, not I, for if I do, he'll be sure to cry.' "

"I'll wake up Little Boy Blue. He knows my voice.

"Cock-a-doodle-do!
Cock-a-doodle-do!
Wake up, wake up,
Little Boy Blue."

Little Boy Blue opened his eyes slowly, sat up, and looked around.

"It must be time for me to get up. Where are my sheep and cow?" he asked.

Then Mother Hen and Gray Squirrel and Dame Duck and Mother Pig and Red Cock called out together:

"Little Boy Blue,
    Come, blow your horn;
    The sheep's in the meadow,
    The cow's in the corn."

Little Boy Blue got up quickly, took his horn, and gave a loud blow. Away ran the sheep out of the meadow and the cow out of the corn.

Then Mother Hen and her little chicks went to the meadow to run and scratch. Gray Squirrel and her little ones frisked about in the clover. Dame Duck and her ducklings went safely through the meadow and had a fine swim in the duck-pond. And Mother Pig grunted to her little ones that they could have a fine roll on the mud-bank after all.

And Red Cock crowed all day,

> "Cock-a-doodle-do!
> I woke Little Boy Blue."

And Little Boy Blue did *not* cry.

LITTLE RED RIDING HOOD

"By the side of a wood, a cottage stood,
   Where a little girl dwelt, who wore a red hood."

Little Red Riding Hood lived in a cottage near a wood. Her grandmother made her a nice, warm, red cloak with a hood. The little girl loved it dearly. She wore it so often that people called her Little Red Riding Hood.

One morning her mother said, "Red Riding Hood, take this cake and pot of butter to your grandmother. Do not stop on the way, for I wish her to have them for dinner. See, I'll put them into this little basket."

Red Riding Hood put on her little cloak and hood. Then taking the basket on her arm she started for her grandmother's cottage.

She had to pass through the thick wood; but she was not afraid because the woodcutters were at work. She tripped along singing merrily.

"Good morning!" said a queer voice. Red Riding

Hood stopped and listened. There stood a wolf. He did not spring at the little girl, because he knew the wood-cutters were near.

"Good morning, Master Wolf," said Little Red Riding Hood, stopping to talk to him. She was not at all afraid.

"Where are you going?" he asked.

"I'm on my way to my grandmother's," she answered, very politely.

"Oh, indeed," said the wolf. "May I ask where your grandmother lives?"

"She lives all alone in a little cottage on the other side of the wood," said Little Red Riding Hood.

"And you are taking her something nice to eat, I see," said the wolf, looking into the basket.

"Yes, mother is sending her a cake and a pot of fresh butter."

"I'll walk a little way with you, my friend," said the wolf. "Will you tell me your name?"

"I'm called Little Red Riding Hood."

"Of course! Your cloak and hood are bright red. Does your grandmother know that you are bringing her some nice things to eat?"

"Oh, no! But I'll tell her before I open the door and go in."

"And how does she know it is her Little Red Riding Hood who has come?"

"When I reach granny's cottage I always take care
To knock at the door till she calls out, 'Who's there?'
'Your grandchild, who brings you a bite and a sup
From her mother,' say I;
And she's sure to reply,
'If you'll pull at the bobbin, the latch will fly up.'"

"I see," nodded the wolf. Then he added, "Well, good day to you, Little Red Riding Hood. I am going to take this path."

As soon as he was hidden by the trees he swam across a pond and took the shortest way to the cottage.

Tap! tap! tap! The wolf knocked on the door with his paw.

No one answered. He rapped again. No one answered. He rapped again. Then he pulled at the bobbin and the latch went up.

The wolf went inside. Granny was not at home. She had gone to the nearest village to see a sick friend.

How disappointed that wolf was! Then he thought, "Red Riding Hood will be here soon. I will wait for her."

He seized the old lady's nightcap which lay upon the bed, and put it on his head. Then he jumped into bed, drew the bedclothes close under his chin, and waited for Little Red Riding Hood to come.

It was some time before she reached the cottage. She had stopped to gather a bouquet for her grandmother.

Tap! tap! tap!

"Who's there?" called out a gruff voice.

"What a bad cold grandmother has," thought the little girl. But she said, "Your grandchild, who brings you a bite and a sup from her mother."

"If you pull at the bobbin the latch will fly up," answered the wolf.

She pulled at the bobbin and the latch flew up. Then she went inside.

"Put your basket on the table, dear, and come to me," said the wolf.

Little Red Riding Hood did as she was told. When

she stood by the bedside she said, "Why, grandmother, what long arms you have!"

"The better to hug you with, my dear," said the wolf.

"And, grandmother, what long ears you have!"

"The better to hear you with, my dear."

"But what big eyes you have!"

"The better to see you with, my dear."

"But, grandmother, what big teeth you have!"

"The better to eat you with, my dear!"

Up he sprang; and Little Red Riding Hood gave a loud scream. A woodcutter who was passing rushed into the cottage and killed the wolf with his axe.

Just as he did so, Granny came home and heard the story of the wicked wolf. Then she and Little Red Riding Hood sat down and had tea together.

LITTLE TINKLE-TOO AND THE SHEPHERD BOY

Once there was a Brownie called Little Tinkle-too. He lived in a little house under the ground. Many other Brownies lived near him.

At night they often came up to make merry under the trees. The little fellows always danced in green suits and glass shoes. And each wore a red, pointed cap, with a little silver bell on it.

They had to take great care of their caps and bells. If a Brownie lost his cap he was sad, indeed. If he lost his bell he could not sleep day or night until he found it.

Little Tinkle-too loved his red cap so much that he wore it everywhere he went. You could hear his bell's tinkle day and night. That is why the other Brownies called him Little Tinkle-too.

One night they were making merry under the trees. As they danced Little Tinkle-too lost his bell. It fell off and lay in the grass.

At first he did not miss it. But when he reached home he found his little silver bell gone. He ran to the other Brownies crying:

> "What shall I do?
> What shall I do?
> For I have lost
> My tinkle-too!"

"You must look for it, Little Tinkle-too," said one.

"You cannot dance in the ring until you have found it," said the others.

Little Tinkle-too looked and looked for his bell; but he could not find it.

"Perhaps a bird has found my tinkle-too. Magpies like shining things. One may have carried it to his nest."

So Little Tinkle-too changed himself into a bird. He flew up into the trees and peeped into each nest. There was no bell in any of them. Then he felt very sad. He spread out his wings and flew over the meadow calling out,

> "What shall I do?
> What shall I do?
> Who has seen my tinkle-too?"

At last he heard below him the sound of tinkling bells. He looked down. There he saw a flock of sheep. Some of the sheep had bells at their necks. They tinkled merrily as the sheep trotted about.

"Now I shall find my little bell," said the Brownie.

He flew round and round above the heads of the sheep, singing to each,

"Little sheep, little sheep,

Tell me if my bell you keep.

If you have my tinkle-too,

No sheep is so rich as you."

A little shepherd boy was watching the sheep. When he heard Little Tinkle-too's song he looked up.

"What a queer bird," he said. "And what does he mean by that strange song? He sings about my sheeps' bells. I have a little silver bell and he doesn't sing about me."

He took the bell out of his pocket and rang it. Tinkle-too! Tinkle-too!

As soon as the Brownie heard that he knew it was the tinkle of his little bell.

"I must think of a way to get it," he said.

So he flew behind a bush, took off his feather dress, and changed himself into an old woman.

The old woman hobbled up to the shepherd boy.

"Good day, lad," she said. "What a pretty bell you have. Will you sell it to me? I will give you three pieces of silver for it."

"No," said the boy, "this bell is not for sale. There is not such another bell in all the world. I have only to give a little tinkle and my sheep go wherever I wish. What a sweet sound it has! Only listen!" He rang the bell two or three times.

"It has indeed a sweet sound. I will give you five pieces of gold for it."

The lad shook his head.

"Then perhaps you will sell it for this." She held out her hand full of gold.

"No, no," said the boy. "I do not want money. Gold is nothing to a bell like this."

The old woman saw that the shepherd boy would not sell the bell for money. So she tried another way of getting it.

"See this pretty white stick. If you had it for your

shepherd's staff, you would always do well. Your sheep would never wander away and get lost. Every year they would give you more wool than any other sheep in these meadows."

The lad looked at the stick. It was white and it had many pictures of shepherds and sheep and lambs on it.

"Look at it, boy. I will give it to you for the bell," she said. The shepherd boy took the stick and looked at it carefully. "It would make a good staff for me," he thought. Then to the old woman he said, "Very well, the stick for the bell!"

As soon as the old woman got the bell she changed herself into a little bird once more. Then like a breath of wind the little bird flew away.

As soon as he reached the Brownies' home he threw off his feather dress and was Little Tinkle-too once more.

"Hurrah! I've found my tinkle-too,
Now I'll dance again with you!"

The shepherd boy kept the stick and used it as a staff. From that time no other sheep in the land did so well as his.

THE SPARROW AND THE CROW

A sparrow and a crow agreed to have a pudding for dinner. The sparrow brought rice and the crow brought raisins. The sparrow was the cook.

When the pudding was ready, the sparrow looked at the crow.

"How dirty you are," he said. "Your body is quite black. Your head looks as if it were covered with coal dust and ashes. Go and wash in the pond first. When you are clean you may share this pudding with me."

So the crow went to the pond and said:

"Your name, sir, is pond,
But my name is crow.
Please give me some water;
For if you do so
I can wash beak and feet
And the nice pudding eat.
128

Though I really don't know
What the sparrow can mean;
For I'm sure, as crows go,
I'm remarkably clean!"

The pond said, "I will give you water. First you must go to the deer. Beg him to give you a horn. Then with it you can dig a little rill for the water to flow in clean and fresh."

So the crow flew to the deer and said:

"Your name, sir, is deer,
But my name is crow.
Please give me a horn;
For if you do so
I can dig a clean rill
For the water to fill.
Then I'll wash beak and feet
And the nice pudding eat.
Though I really don't know
What the sparrow can mean;
For I'm sure, as crows go,
I'm remarkably clean."

But the deer said, "I will give you a horn. But first you must go to the cow. Ask her to give you some milk for me to drink."

So the crow flew off to the cow and said:

> "Your name, ma'am, is cow,
> But my name is crow.
> Please give me some milk;
> For if you do so
> The deer in his turn
> Will give me his horn,
> And I'll dig a clean rill
> For the water to fill.
> Then I'll wash beak and feet
> And the nice pudding eat.
> Though I really don't know
> What the sparrow can mean;
> For I'm sure, as crows go,
> I'm remarkably clean."

The cow said, "I will give you milk. But first you must bring me some grass."

So the crow flew to the grass and said:

"Your name, sir, is grass,

But my name is crow.

Please give me some blades;

For if you do so

The cow will give milk

To the deer sleek as silk,

And he in his turn

Will give me his horn,

And I'll dig a clean rill

For the water to fill.

Then I'll wash beak and feet

And the nice pudding eat.

Though I really don't know

What the sparrow can mean;

For I'm sure, as crows go,

I'm remarkably clean."

The grass said, "I will give you some blades. But first you must go to the blacksmith. Ask him to make you a sickle. Then you can cut me."

So the crow went to the blacksmith and said:

"Your name, sir, is smith,

But my name is crow.

Please give me a sickle;

For if you do so

The grass I can mow

As food for the cow.

The cow will give milk

To the deer sleek as silk,

And he in his turn

Will give me his horn,

And I'll dig a clean rill

For the water to fill;

Then I'll wash beak and feet

And the nice pudding eat.

Though I really don't know

What the sparrow can mean;

For I'm sure, as crows go,

I'm remarkably clean."

The blacksmith said, "I will give you a sickle if you will put the coal on the fire, then light it, and blow the bellows."

So the crow began to put the coal on the fire. In so doing he fell among the coals. Then he began to light the fire and blow the bellows. But the bellows blew him up the blacksmith's chimney. And when the crow looked at himself he was blacker than ever.

So the sparrow ate all the nice pudding.

A CLEVER MOUSE

Mrs. Mouse and her three little mice sat before the fire one day.

"My children," said Mrs. Mouse, "you are now old enough to take care of yourselves. Would you like to build houses of your own?"

"Yes, yes, mother," squeaked the three. "Please let us build houses of our own."

"Very well," said their mother. "I will hear your lesson once more before you go. Tell me who likes to eat mice."

"The cat," called out the three.

"Say that again," said Mrs. Mouse.

"The cat likes to eat mice."

"What should you do when you see a cat coming?"

"Run," said Squeak.

"Run at once," said Peek.

"Run at once, if you get the chance," said Sleek.

"Oh, Little Sleek," said his mother. "If you don't get

the chance, *make* it. Now go and build good, strong houses."

"Hurrah! hurrah! a little house for each of us!"

And away scampered the three mice.

Each built the kind of house he liked best. Squeak's house was made of hay. He said hay would keep him warm. Peek made his house of straw. He thought straw better than hay for building.

"I shall have a brick house," said Sleek. "Nothing like brick for me." So he built himself a brick house.

One day Squeak heard a knock at his door.

"Who's there?" he called out.

"A friend. Let me come in!"

The voice was very sweet.

"You are the cat. You may not come into my house," called out Squeak.

Puss pushed her paw into the hay house. And that was the end of poor Squeak.

Puss went to the next house and knocked at the door.

"Who's there?" asked Peek.

"A friend. Let me come in!"

This time the voice was very, very sweet.

"You are the cat. You may not come into my house," called out Peek.

Then Puss pushed her paw into the straw house. And that was the end of poor Peek.

Puss went on to the next house and knocked. No one answered. Then she knocked and knocked and knocked. No one answered. Sleek was not at home.

"I will wait," said Puss.

Soon Sleek came creeping along quietly. Puss saw him, but he did not see her at his door. In a moment she had him under her paws. He hadn't even a chance to run.

"Puss," said Sleek, "you have caught me. Are you going to eat me?"

"I am," said Puss.

"You must wash your face first," said Sleek. "All polite people wash their faces before eating."

Puss waited a moment.

"Very well," she said. "I will wash my face first. Then I will eat you."

She lifted her paw. Away ran Sleek into his house.

Puss tried and tried to get in but she could not move that brick house.

"Mother was right," said Sleek. "If you don't get a chance to run, *make* one!"

"Humph," said Puss when she had given up. "The next time I shall wash my face *after* eating."

THE USEFUL POKER

"Ha! ha! ha!" laughed Old Poker. "Ha! ha! ha!"

"What are you laughing at? I was almost asleep," snapped Polished Tongs.

"Please excuse me, sir," said Old Poker meekly. "I really couldn't help it. Whenever I think about the merry games the children played this afternoon, I feel as happy as a cricket. And how pretty the dancing was, too. I believe I like the minuet best. It is so old-fashioned, and the lads and lassies dance it very gracefully."

"Well, I should think you would be too tired to feel merry. You were in use the whole afternoon," said Polished Tongs.

"Yes, indeed! It was a busy afternoon for me. But the beauty of an open fire is a cheery blaze; so you see I'm needed very often to stir up the coals," replied Old Poker.

"Well, I must say you're more cheerful than I could be if my back were as bent as yours is," added Shovel, laughingly. "And your head is a little on one side, isn't it?

Dear me! What a pity! You are very much over-worked."

"Oh! I don't mind it in the least," said Old Poker.

"Well, I heard the mistress of the house say yesterday that you were almost worn out and that you would be stored in the attic soon," snapped Polished Tongs. "So you see what comes of being so useful! Now it is quite likely that Shovel and I will stand here on the open hearth for many seasons to come." Polished Tongs looked admiringly at his bright legs.

"We are indeed worth looking at," nodded Shovel, straightening up.

"Yes, you are both very bright and handsome, to be sure," sighed Old Poker, a little sorrowfully.

The next morning the children were eagerly waiting for their mother to come into the sitting-room, for they had bought a set of new-fashioned andirons for her birth-day gift. The old set, tongs, shovel, and poker had been taken to a lumber room in the attic and stored away.

Of course mother was very much surprised and de-lighted with her gift; but when the family gathered about the hearth father said, "Come, we must have a cheery blaze on mother's birthday." He reached forward to take the new poker in order to stir up the coals.

"Oh! please don't use the new poker. You'll make it dull," said mother.

"All right, but I must have a cheery blaze," laughed father. "Where is my Old Poker?"

"In the attic," cried the children.

"Then I'll fetch him down and keep him on my side of the hearth," laughed father.

He hurried away to the attic and brought back with him Old Poker, who enjoyed many a pleasant season in the sitting-room, while Polished Tongs and Shovel rusted away in the attic.

WHY THE BANANA BELONGS TO THE MONKEY

Perhaps you do not know it, but when Brazilian children eat bananas they say, "I am a monkey." I once knew a little boy in Brazil who was very, very fond of bananas. He always said, "I am very much of a monkey." If you are fond of bananas these children would tell you that you are a monkey, too. This is the story they tell to show us how it all came about.

Once upon a time when the world had just been made and there was only one kind of banana, but very many kinds of monkeys, there was a little old woman who had a big garden full of banana trees. It was hard for the old woman to gather the bananas herself, so she made a bargain with the largest monkey.

She told him that if he would gather the bunches of bananas for her she would give him half of them. So the monkey gathered the bananas. But when he took his half, he gave the little old woman those which grew at the bottom of the bunch and were small and wrinkled. The nice big fat ones he kept for himself and carried them home to let them ripen in the dark.

The little old woman was very angry. She lay awake all night trying to think of some plan by which she could punish the monkey for his selfishness. At last she thought of a way.

The next morning she made an image of wax, which looked just like a little boy. Then she placed a large flat basket on the top of the image's head, and in the basket she put the best ripe bananas she could find. They looked very tempting.

After a while the biggest monkey passed that way. He saw the image of wax and thought that it was a boy peddling bananas. He had often played tricks on boys who sold bananas. Sometimes he had upset their baskets, and had run away with the fruit. This morning the biggest monkey was feeling very good-natured, so he thought that he would first try asking politely for the bananas.

"O peddler boy, peddler boy," he said, "please give me a banana." The image of wax answered never a word.

Then the monkey called out in his loudest voice, "O

peddler boy, peddler boy, if you don't give me a banana I'll give you such a push that it will upset all the fruit in your basket." The image of wax was silent. The monkey ran toward the image and struck it hard with his hand. His hand stuck fast.

"O peddler boy, peddler boy, let go my hand," the monkey called out. "Let go my hand and give me a banana, or I'll give you a hard, hard blow with my other hand."

The wax image did not let go.

The monkey gave the image a hard, hard blow with his other hand. The other hand stuck fast, too. Then the monkey called out, "O peddler boy, peddler boy, let go my two hands. Let go and give me a banana, or I'll give you a kick with my foot."

But the wax image did not let go.

The monkey gave the image a kick with his foot, and his foot stuck fast in the wax.

"O peddler boy, peddler boy," the monkey cried, "let go my foot. Let go my two hands and my foot and give me a banana, or I'll give you a kick with my other foot."

The wax image did not let go.

Then the monkey, who was now very angry, gave the image of wax a kick with his other foot and that foot stuck fast, too.

The monkey shouted, "O peddler boy, peddler boy, let go my foot. Let go my two feet and my two hands and give me a banana, or I'll give you a push with my body."

But the image did not let go.

The monkey gave the image of wax a push with his body, and his body caught fast, too.

"O peddler boy, peddler boy," the monkey shouted, "Let go my body, and my two feet and my two hands, or I'll call all the other monkeys to help me!"

But the image of wax did not let go.

Then the monkey made such a noise with his cries and shouts that very soon many monkeys came running from every direction. There were big monkeys and little monkeys and middle-sized monkeys. A whole army of them had come to help the biggest monkey.

It was the very little monkey who thought of a plan to help the biggest monkey out of his trouble. He told the monkeys to climb up into the tallest tree and pile themselves one on top of another, until they made a pyramid of monkeys. The monkey with the loudest voice of all was to be on top, and he was to shout his very loudest to the sun and ask it to come and help the biggest monkey out of his trouble.

Then all the big-sized, little-sized, and middle-sized monkeys did what the littlest monkey planned. And the monkey with the loudest voice on top of the pyramid made the sun hear what they wanted. The sun came at once and poured its hot rays down upon the wax image. After a while the wax began to melt. The monkey, which was stuck fast, was at last able to pull out one of his hands. The sun poured down more of his hot rays, and soon the monkey was able to pull out the other hand. Then he pulled out one foot; then the other, and in a little while he loosened his body, too. At last he was free.

When the little old woman saw what had happened she was very much discouraged about raising bananas. She made up her mind to move to another part of the world where she could raise cabbages instead. The monkeys were left with the big garden full of banana trees. And from that day to this, the monkeys have thought that they own all the bananas in the world.

So you see that if you like bananas, you are a little monkey.

LITTLE TUPPENS

Once upon a time there lived an old hen whose name was Cluck-cluck. One day she said to her little chick, Tuppens:

"Come, we will go to the woods and get some blueberries for breakfast."

Tuppens ate the blueberries too fast and one stuck in his throat and choked him.

Off ran poor Cluck-cluck to fetch her chick some water. She ran to the Spring and said:

"Dear Spring, please give me water.
 A blueberry is stuck fast
 In my little Tuppens' throat!
 He is choking!"

The Spring said: "I will give you some water, old hen, if you will fetch me a cup."

Cluck-cluck ran to the Oak tree and said:

"Dear old Oak tree, please give me an acorn-cup.

> I will take the cup to the Spring.
> The Spring will give me water.
> A blueberry is stuck fast
> In my little Tuppens' throat!
> He is choking!"

The Oak tree said: "I will give you an acorn-cup, old hen, if some one will shake my branches."

Cluck-cluck ran to the woodcutter's little Elsa and said:

"Dear little Elsa, please shake old Oak tree's branches.

Old Oak tree will give me an acorn-cup.

> I will take the cup to the Spring.
> The Spring will give me water.
> A blueberry is stuck fast
> In my little Tuppens' throat!
> He is choking!"

The woodcutter's little Elsa said: "I will shake Oak tree's branches, old hen, if you will fetch me some shoes."

Cluck-cluck ran to the Shoemaker and said:

"Dear Shoemaker, please give me shoes,

Shoes for the woodcutter's little Elsa.

Then little Elsa will shake old Oak tree's branches.

Old Oak tree will give me an acorn-cup.

I will take the cup to the Spring.
The Spring will give me water.
A blueberry is stuck fast
In my little Tuppens' throat!
He is choking!"

The Shoemaker said: "I will give you shoes, old hen, if you will fetch me leather."

Cluck-cluck ran to Red Ox and said:
"Dear Red Ox, please give me leather for the Shoe-
maker.
Then the Shoemaker will make little Elsa's shoes.
Little Elsa will shake old Oak tree's branches.
Old Oak tree will give me an acorn-cup.

I will take the cup to the Spring.
The Spring will give me water.
A blueberry is stuck fast
In my little Tuppens' throat!
He is choking!"

Red Ox said: "I will give you leather if you will fetch me corn to eat."

Cluck-cluck ran to the Farmer and said:

"Dear Farmer, please give me corn for Red Ox.

Then Red Ox will give leather to the Shoemaker.

The Shoemaker will make little Elsa's shoes.

Little Elsa will shake old Oak tree's branches.

Old Oak tree will give me an acorn-cup.

I will take the cup to the Spring.

The Spring will give me water.

A blueberry is stuck fast

In my little Tuppens' throat!

He is choking!"

The Farmer said: "I will give you some corn if you will fetch me a plow."

Cluck-cluck ran to the Blacksmith and said:

"Dear Blacksmith, please give me a plow for the Farmer.

Then the Farmer will give corn to Red Ox.

Red Ox will give leather to the Shoemaker.

The Shoemaker will make little Elsa's shoes.

Little Elsa will shake old Oak tree's branches.

Old Oak tree will give me an acorn-cup.

I will take the cup to the Spring.
The Spring will give me water.
A blueberry is stuck fast
In my little Tuppens' throat!
He is choking!"

The Blacksmith said: "I will give you a plow if you will fetch me some iron."

Cluck-cluck ran to the busy little Dwarfs who live in the mountains, and said:

"Dear busy little Dwarfs, please give me some iron for
the Blacksmith.
Then the Blacksmith will make a plow for the Farmer.
The Farmer will give corn to Red Ox.
Red Ox will give leather to the Shoemaker.
The Shoemaker will make little Elsa's shoes.
Little Elsa will shake old Oak tree's branches.
Old Oak tree will give me an acorn-cup.

I will take the cup to the Spring.
The Spring will give me water.
A blueberry is stuck fast
In my little Tuppens' throat!
He is choking!"

The busy little Dwarfs said: "Poor Cluck-cluck! Poor little Tuppens!"

Then they gave the old hen a heap of iron.

Cluck-cluck gave the iron to the Blacksmith.

The Blacksmith gave a plow to the Farmer.

The Farmer gave corn to Red Ox,

Red Ox gave leather to the Shoemaker.

The Shoemaker made shoes for little Elsa.

Little Elsa shook old Oak tree's branches.

Old Oak tree gave an acorn-cup.

The Spring filled the cup with water.

Cluck-cluck ran to the woods with the water,

Little Tuppens drank the water.

Then away he ran to play.

LITTLE BUTTERFLY'S DIAMOND

Once upon a time there was a fairy called Little Butterfly. Some one had given her that name because she had beautiful green wings with silver spots on them.

But Little Butterfly would do no work. She liked best to play all day long, or to sleep curled up in the heart of a blossom. Oh, she was a lazy little fairy!

The queen of the fairies knew Little Butterfly's faults and wished to help her correct them. So one day the queen commanded Little Butterfly to go to a country which was far away.

"You are to stay there until you have made a beautiful diamond. It must be more beautiful than any a fairy has ever worn."

When Little Butterfly heard this she bowed her head but she said nothing. As soon as she was alone she burst into a flood of tears.

"To make a diamond is an endless task. Every day for years and years I must turn it over with my wand. Oh, I am a most unhappy fairy."

She sat down and cried for many minutes. Then up she jumped and stamped her little feet on the ground.

"I won't do it! I shall run away to the air fairies," she exclaimed. "They will think me beautiful and not make me work. Such a little fairy as I am can never make a diamond."

Then she peeped into the brook to admire herself. Alas! She saw that the beautiful green of her wings had faded and the silver spots were all dim. If fairies have naughty hearts, their wings droop and their beauty fades. At sight of herself Little Butterfly wept aloud with anger and shame.

"The queen thinks I won't go away looking like this; but I will. I'll go just to let her see that I do not care about her."

As she spoke the silver spots left her beautiful wings and they became a dirty brown. She waved her wand and called out angrily,

"Humming Bird, Humming Bird, come nigh! come nigh!
And carry me off to the far blue sky!"

In a moment a tiny humming bird was at her feet.

Little Butterfly jumped upon the bird's back and away they flew to the golden clouds of the west. There the queen of the air and her fairies had their palace.

As Little Butterfly drew near the cloud palace the queen and her fairies caught sight of a pair of dirty brown wings. The air fairies waved their wands and were to be seen no more.

Little Butterfly found herself alone in the palace. And such a beautiful one as it was! The clouds hung round it like wonderful curtains and the floor was a rainbow. Many beautiful birds fluttered in the sunlight. Their sweet voices filled the palace with sweet sounds. Little Butterfly, tired from her journey, lay down on a rosy cloud and fell fast asleep.

When she awoke she saw a bird building its nest beside her. Straw after straw the little thing brought in her bill. Then she wove them together for her nest.

"She is a foolish little thing to work so hard. She'll never finish it," thought the fairy.

But the little bird worked away busily and the nest was soon finished. When Little Butterfly peeped into it she called out, "Oh, what a pretty thing!"

In a moment she heard a voice singing,

"Little by little the bird builds her nest."

She started up. Before her stood the queen of the air fairies.

"Foolish fairy, we allow no idlers here. Go and make your diamond. Then you will be welcome. Remember that time and patience will accomplish all things.

"Little by little the bird builds her nest."

Before Little Butterfly could say a word the queen was gone.

Butterfly began now to feel ashamed of being so lazy. But she did not yet wish to make the diamond. So she waved her wand and called the humming bird once more and away they flew. Soon they alighted close to a little green hill where her own queen lived.

Near the hill Butterfly saw some bees at work. She watched them slip into the flowers, gather the honey, and fly back with it to their hive.

"I wish I loved to be busy as they do. But I can not think of making that diamond. I should never finish it."

Then she heard fairy voices singing,

"Little by little the bee builds her cell!"

Butterfly knew the voices came from her fairy sisters. She wished she were at home dancing on the green with them.

"I will make the diamond," she said. "I shall finish it some time. Then I can fly home every evening and dance in the fairy ring."

But when Little Butterfly began to think of the hard work she must do she stamped her little feet again and said, "I never can do it. I'll go to the queen of the ocean fairies. I am sure she will let me live with her and do no work there."

No sooner had she said these words than away she ran to the seashore. When she reached the beach she called out,

"Argonaut! Argonaut! Come to me
And carry me through the cold green sea!"

Soon a little boat came floating over the waters toward Butterfly. As it neared the shore a wave landed it safely at the fairy's feet. She stepped into it and away the boat sped with her down, down, down to the bed of the ocean. There before her eyes stood the wonderful coral palace of the ocean fairies

When the queen and the ocean fairies saw Butterfly's dirty wings they waved their wands and were seen no more.

Again Little Butterfly found herself alone in a wonderful palace. Pink coral pillars were twisted in many beautiful forms. Pearls hung among the branches. Sea moss made cool deep seats on a sandy floor covered with many colored shells.

"Oh, how beautiful it all is. Giants must have made those coral pillars," exclaimed Little Butterfly.

As she spoke she saw thousands of tiny insects on a coral pillar near her. While she looked and wondered she heard voices singing,

"Little by little the insects build our coral bowers."

Nearer and nearer came the sound. In a moment thousands of fairies came toward her floating through the water on beautiful shells. In the largest shell was the queen.

"Foolish fairy," said the queen when she saw Little Butterfly. "We allow no idlers here. Look at the pillars of my palace. They were made by creatures smaller than yourself. Labor and patience did it all."

The queen waved her wand and the shells floated away.

"All creatures are busy on the earth, in the air, and in the water," thought Little Butterfly. "And they all seem to be happy at their work. Perhaps I can learn to be so, too. I'll make the diamond and it shall be as beautiful as a sunbeam."

So Little Butterfly went to the country where her queen had sent her. Day by day she worked at her task. In a short time her wings became a beautiful green and the silver spots were so bright that they seemed like sparks of fire. Never had she been so happy. Never had she been so loved by all.

Seven years passed away. One day the queen of the fairies saw a bright little creature come to her and kneel at her feet. The stranger offered a gift which gave light like a star. Then the queen knew that her visitor was Little Butterfly and the gift was Little Butterfly's diamond.

TOM THUMB

In the days of good King Arthur, there lived a plough-man and his wife, who wished very much to have a son; so the man went to Merlin the enchanter, and asked him to let him have a child even if it were *"no bigger than his thumb."*

"Go home and you will find one," said Merlin; and when the man came back to his house he found his wife nursing a very, very wee baby, who in four minutes grew to the size of the ploughman's thumb, and never grew any more. The fairy queen came to his christening, and named him "Tom Thumb." She then dressed him nicely in a shirt of spider's web and a doublet and a hose of thistledown.

One day, while Tom's mother was making a plum pud-ding, Tom stood on the edge of the bowl with a lighted candle in his hand, that she might see to make it properly. Unfortunately, however, while her back was turned, Tom fell into the bowl, and his mother not missing him, stirred him up in the pudding, and put it and him into the pot.

Tom no sooner felt the hot water than he danced about like mad; the woman was nearly frightened out of her wits to see the pudding come out of the pot and jump about, and she was glad to give it to a tinker who was passing that way.

The tinker was delighted with his present; but as he was getting over a stile, he happened to sneeze very hard, and Tom called out from the middle of the pudding, "Hullo, Pickens!" which so terrified the tinker that he threw the pudding into the field, and scampered away as fast as he could. The pudding tumbled to pieces in the fall and Tom, creeping out, went home to his mother, who was in great affliction because she could not find him.

A few days afterward Tom went with his mother into the fields to milk the cows, and for fear he should be blown away by the wind, she tied him to a thistle with a small piece of thread. Very soon after, a cow ate the thistle and swallowed Tom Thumb. His mother was in sad grief again; but Tom scratched and kicked in the cow's throat till she was glad to throw him out of her mouth again.

One day Tom went ploughing with his father, who gave him a whip made of a barley straw, to drive the oxen with; but an eagle flying by caught him up in his beak, and carried him to the top of a great giant's castle. The giant would have eaten Tom up; but the fairy dwarf scratched and bit his tongue and held on by his teeth till the giant in a passion took him out again and threw him into the sea, where a very large fish swallowed him up directly. The fish was caught soon after and sent as a present to King Arthur, and when the cook opened it there was Tom Thumb inside. He was carried to the king, who was delighted with the little man. Tom walked on the king's left hand, and danced on the queen's. He became a great favorite with Arthur, who made him a knight.

THE FAIRY'S BEST GIFT

Once upon a time there lived a King and Queen who had an only daughter. They loved her dearly. She had two godmothers, a Red Fairy and a Blue Fairy. When this royal baby was christened the two fairies came to see it. Each brought a wonderful gift.

The Red Fairy said, "I bring the Princess a pearl of great worth, and three other gifts. They are beauty, wealth, and wisdom. So long as she wears this jewel she will grow prettier, richer, and wiser every day. But should she lose the pearl, the other three gifts will leave her. She will not recover them until she finds the lost gem."

The Blue Fairy said, "The little Princess has received wonderful gifts. But I have brought one which is better than them all. So long as she keeps the pearl my gift will be of no value. But should she lose your gifts, she will receive mine. I will give her a humble heart."

Then the two fairies nodded and went away.

The King and Queen were delighted with the Red Fairy's gift. His majesty said, "We'll take good care of the pearl. She can do without the Blue Fairy's gift. If our little Princess be beautiful, rich, and wise it matters little about her heart."

"Yes, to be sure," said the Queen. "A humble heart, indeed! What has a princess to do with such a gift!"

Then the King had a gold crown made for the little Princess. The wonder of it was that the crown grew as the child grew, so that it always fitted her head. No one else could wear it. At the top of this crown was safely set the beautiful pearl.

The Princess never took her crown off. She wore it day and night. Indeed, the King and Queen were so afraid of her losing it that they chose eight servants to guard the child and the pearl.

So the Princess grew up and everything happened as the Red Fairy had said. The maiden was indeed the loveliest princess in all the world. Her eyes shone like stars and she was as fair as a flower. She lived in a beautiful palace. The floor of her room was silver and pearl. On the walls hung costly mirrors and the ceiling was made of rare gems. She was so clever that she could remember the longest lesson if she read it but once. Indeed, all the wise men of her father's kingdom came to talk with her. They all said that she was the most wonderful princess that they had ever met. On all sides the Princess heard her own praises sung. At last, I am sorry to say, she grew very proud.

One day when she was about fifteen years old the Princess went walking in the royal gardens. When she reached the park gate she turned to her servants and said, "I wish to go beyond the gate. Unlock it."

"Oh! my dear Princess," said one of the servants. "We dare not." But the Princess laughed scornfully and said, "Then I shall do as I please about it."

She climbed quickly over the gate and ran away through the woods. The servants tried to follow her but she went so swiftly that she was soon lost among the trees.

After she had traveled a long distance the Princess felt tired and thirsty, so she sat down to rest by a spring. She stooped over to quench her thirst and saw herself in the clear water.

"How beautiful I am," she said. "How wonderfully

beautiful I am!" Then she slowly bent her head nearer and nearer to the water. Splash! Something tumbled into the spring. For a moment she could not think what had happened. She put her hand up to her head. Then she knew that her crown had fallen off. She looked into the spring to see what had become of it, but she could find no trace of it. And to her surprise she no longer saw the picture of a lovely princess in the clear water. Instead, she saw the image of a poor bare-footed girl dressed in rags. She could not remember who she was, where she had come from, nor where she was going. Away she ran from the spring, deeper and deeper into the forest.

Finally, the child came to a little cottage and knocked at the door. An old woman opened it, and said, "Poor child! Where do you come from at this late hour?"

The Princess burst into tears and said, "I do not know."

The old woman felt sorry for the child.

"You are poor and lonely," she said. "Come in. I need some one to take care of my goats. If you are kind and helpful and are willing to live on bread and water you may stay with me."

"I am thankful to live with you and take care of your

goats," said the Princess, kissing the old woman's hand.

You see the Blue Fairy had kept her word. When the crown was lost she gave the Princess, in its place, a humble heart.

There was great grief at the Royal Palace when the King and Queen heard that the Princess had disappeared. Throughout the land they sent word that any man who found the lost Princess should have her for his bride. Also, they added, he should have half the kingdom.

Many noble youths hoped to win the lost Princess. For three long years they searched far and near, but they did not find her.

One bright morning a handsome prince rode up to the door of the old woman's cottage.

"Why do you wear that black dress, good mother?" asked the youth.

"The King has commanded everyone to wear mourning for the lost Princess," she replied. "But I'm sure she was no great loss, for the people say she had a very proud heart."

Just then appeared a meek young girl with a herd of

goats. The moment the Prince saw the young shepherdess, he loved her. He forgot about his search for the lost Princess. Instead of returning to the King's court he built a castle in the woods and made his home there.

One hot day when he was very thirsty he knelt down to drink at a spring. There, shining in the clear depths, was a golden crown with a wonderful pearl set on the top. He drew it out of the water and took it to the Royal Palace. The moment his majesty saw it, he knew it was the crown of the lost Princess.

Of course he feared that the Princess was dead, but he decided, nevertheless, to search a little longer for his lost child. He ordered all girls in the kingdom who were eighteen years old to come to the palace and try on the crown. The one whom it fitted should be the bride of the prince who found it.

Many girls came to the castle to try on the crown; but it fitted none. At last it seemed that every maiden in the kingdom but the good little shepherdess had been to court.

"Let us try the crown on the goat-girl," said the Prince.

"Oh, no! no! no!" everybody at court exclaimed.

But the King said, "Bring the goat-girl to the palace."

There, before all the people, the Prince tried the crown on the shepherdess; and lo! it fitted her head perfectly. The youth said to himself, "This is the maiden whom I loved dearly when I first saw her. I know that sunshine follows wherever she goes."

Then all the people cried out, "Long live the Prince and Princess," but in their hearts they thought, "Surely this goat-girl is *not* the royal Princess." They could not see her very well, for the sun had set and it was dusk.

"The wedding shall take place in the banquet-hall of the castle," declared the King, who was anxious now to see the shepherdess under the light.

They led the goat-girl with the crown on her head into a great hall lighted by thousands of candles. But brighter than all the light shone the beauty of the bride dressed in cloth of gold; for, as soon as she recovered her lost crown she got back all the Red Fairy's other gifts. And best of all, she kept the Blue Fairy's gift as well, namely, a good and humble heart. Now the King and Queen knew that she was, indeed, their lost daughter. She spoke gently to her mother and father and asked them to forgive her for running away. Also, she told the Prince that she wished to reward the old woman of the forest who had taken care of her.

The wedding was celebrated with great rejoicing, and all the people said, "Beautiful is the Red Fairy's gift, the pearl of great price. But wonderful, indeed, is the Blue Fairy's gift, a humble heart."

LITTLE MOUSIE BROWN

He climbed up the candlestick,
The little mousie brown,
To steal and eat tallow;
And he couldn't get down.

He called for his grandma,
But his grandma was in town;
So he doubled himself up into a wheel
And rolled himself down.

FOR WINTER TIME

Beautiful butterflies—red, yellow, and white.
Page 110

Out into a whirl of snow!
Page 175

WINTER FUN

Merry Jean and little Ned,
Happy with their bright new sled!
Thick warm boots, and woollen clothes,
Jack Frost! you can't bite their toes!
You may paint red roses bright
On their fat cheeks, round and white!
Out into a whirl of snow,
Down the hills! Oho! Oho!
Climb the hillside! Ready! Start!
Swift as lightning down, down dart!
A little swerve, a turn, a tumble,
At the foot a snowy bundle.
A scream! a laugh! a shake! a run!
Oh, what merry winter fun!

THE SNOWMAN'S SECRET

Christmastide had come and gone, and little Jack had received the gift that he had longed for all the year. It was a bright, new, yellow sled with his name printed in large red letters on the seat.

"Everybody will know this is my sled, because my name is printed on it," thought Jack.

"Mother," he called, "do you think we shall have snow to-morrow?"

"Yes, Jack," answered his mother. "The paper says that the snow will be two feet deep by to-morrow morning."

"No one shall ride on my new sled," said the little fellow to himself. "I shall go up and down the hills alone."

The next morning the world seemed buried in snow. It was deep enough to rejoice the heart of any little boy or girl.

Jack and his sled were off quite early to the hills, which were but a short distance from Jack's home. He was surprised to find many other children there before him. They had made a very large snowman at the top of the highest hill.

"What fun they are having," said Jack. "This is a fine hill for coasting. It's so high."

Down he went several times. Once in a while he would stop to rest. Then he heard the laughter of the little boys and girls as they went merrily up and down the hills. Each sled held two or three children.

"They all seem to be having more fun than I am," he said as he climbed the highest hill.

"Ha! ha! ha!" laughed the Snowman, "and I know why!"

Jack looked up surprised. He forgot for a moment that it was only a Snowman speaking.

"Why are they merrier than I am?" he asked the Snowman.

"Ha! ha! ha!" laughed the Snowman once more. "That is a secret. But you can learn it. See, there come some little children up the hill. They have no sled. Give them a ride," he said smiling.

Jack thought for a while; then he walked slowly up to

a little girl who had been watching him. Soon they were riding up and down with the others, laughing merrily. Again and again they coasted up and down the hills.

Before going home Jack went to the Snowman and said, "I have found out your secret."

"Ha! ha! ha!" laughed the Snowman, "you found it out, my little man!"

Jack ran home and said, "Mother, I found out the Snowman's secret."

And he told her all that had happened.

"You found out that sharing with others makes us happy," said his mother.

NORTH WIND'S FROLIC

In a large, airy castle on the border of a country far away, lived the King of the Winds with his four children, North Wind, South Wind, East Wind, and West Wind. They were a happy family, for the four children were always making merry with the old Wind King.

North Wind, however, was a boisterous fellow, forever causing disorder, even in their play.

One summer day North Wind said that he was going out of the castle for a frolic.

"Go," called out the King, "but be careful, North Wind, what you do. Your pranks are all very well while you are in the castle here, but out in the world they may do great harm."

"Woo-oo-oo—," was all the King heard in answer, and away blustered North Wind out of the castle to the garden which was near.

The roses and lilies were in bloom, and the ripe peaches hung on the trees ready to be picked.

"Woo-oo-oo—," cried the North Wind in his loudest voice, and in a moment the rose petals were scattered all over the ground, the lilies were broken from their stems, and the ripe peaches dropped down right into the mud.

In the fields he caused even greater damage. He broke the wheat stems and threw the unripe apples down. He tore the leaves from their branches and tossed them about in the air in all directions. Indeed, one old tree he completely uprooted.

The people could stand it no longer. They went to the King of the Winds, who, in his castle had control over the coming and going of all the Winds, and told him what the wicked North Wind had done and how the gardens and fields had suffered from the misery he had caused them.

"I will summon North Wind," said his father. "He shall answer for all this."

When North Wind appeared, the King repeated what the people had said. "Is this true, North Wind?" he asked.

North Wind could not deny it, for the devastated gardens and fields lay before every one's eyes.

"Why did you do it?" asked the King.

"Oh," answered North Wind, "I didn't mean it wickedly. I wanted to play with the roses and the lilies and the peaches—and all the rest. I didn't think I should do them any harm."

"I see," said the King. "If you are such a clumsy fellow, then I dare not let you out for a frolic again. I must keep you a prisoner in the castle the whole summer. In the winter, when there are no more flowers and fruit, you may go out and be as boisterous as you like. I see you are fit only for the time of ice and snow and not for the season of flowers and fruit."

SNOWBALL

What a beautiful morning it was when Ralph and Mary looked out of their bedroom window. The ground was covered with newly fallen snow and the little snowflakes were still piling themselves up in great white masses everywhere. How merrily they danced on the window-pane. "What a good time we have together," they seemed to say.

"It's almost deep enough for a sled, Mary. And, oh, the snowballs we can make!" called out Ralph.

"Yes," said mother, as she came up to help the children dress. "You will have a good time as soon as it is not quite so stormy. I've been playing snowball this morning."

"You, mother?" Mary asked in surprise.

"Yes; and I kept my snowball for you to see. It is down in the kitchen; but you must wait till after break-fast to see it. My snowball will not melt!"

A snowball in the kitchen, and one that would not melt! Did you ever hear of anything so strange?

Breakfast was soon over and mother and the children went to the kitchen. Behind the big stove was a small basket. Ralph stepped up quietly and peeped in. Sure enough, it did look as though a white snowball was lying there, and it was only when the white ball raised its head and looked with two sleepy little eyes right at Mary, that she said, "Oh, it's a little white kitten. Where did it come from?"

Then mother told them how, when she had opened the door that morning, the kitten had stepped inside. "At first I thought it was only a drift of snow blown in by wind. But when I saw the little shivering form, I knew what it was. Then I gave it something to eat and made a bed for it, as you see. Do you not think my snowball beautiful?"

"May we keep it?" asked Ralph.

"I feel sure," said mother, "that it has a home. It must belong to some little girl or boy in the neighborhood. When the storm is over we'll try to find its real home." But the merry flakes seemed in no hurry to stop, for they came flying down all day long.

These little flakes fell cold and heavy on the spirits of

one little girl not far from Ralph's and Mary's home. She was thinking about her little kitty. It had left home when the pretty white flakes began to fall, and the little girl had not seen her kitten since. It must surely be lost, for the snow was now quite deep, and kitty was very small. The tears would come into Elsie's eyes. "Perhaps kitty will get hungry," she thought, "and then she'll be glad to come home."

It was late in the afternoon before the storm stopped. Elsie was not long in putting on her hood and mittens. Then she began to search for her kitten. She had not gone far before she saw Mary and Ralph coming toward her with kitty quietly curled up in Mary's arm. Elsie clapped her hands with joy when she saw them.

Then Mary told Elsie how kitty had come in the snow and had to leave them, just as the snow would soon do. Kitty found a very cozy place on Elsie's arm and perhaps she did feel a little more at home there.

"Wouldn't Snowball be a good name for her?" asked Mary.

"Yes, it would," said Elsie, "I have called her Kitty. Snowball shall be her real name."

Elsie thanked the children for their kindness. With Snowball in her arms she ran home a very happy little girl.

THE OLD WOMAN PICKING
HER GEESE

Little old woman up in the sky—
See how she makes the feathers fly!
She sits in the twilight overhead
And picks her geese for a featherbed.
The gray geese flap their heavy wings,
And the little old woman sits and sings:
"How strange that people down below
Should call my bits of feather, snow!"

HOW THE TREES KEPT CHRISTMAS

One Christmas Eve the trees in a wood were very un-happy. They wished very much to keep Christmas, but they did not know how to do so.

"We look so brown," said one.

"And so bare," said another.

"If we only had our pretty green summer dresses," said a third, "then we should be decorated and could keep Christmas."

"Hush! children, hush!" whispered North Wind in quite a gentle voice for such a rough fellow. "Make haste and go to sleep."

"Hush! children, hush!" softly murmured a sleepy little bird. He was roosting on one of the branches of the unhappy trees.

So the trees dropped off to sleep, one by one, while a little star twinkled peacefully overhead.

But while they slept something happened. And when

the trees awoke they found that some one, perhaps North Wind, had, during the night, cast over each of them a lovely soft cloak of spotless feathery white.

"How beautiful we are!" said the trees. "Now we can keep our Christmas!"

A CHRISTMAS CRAFT

"Hullo," said the Moon, "what is this?"

She was sailing out from the clouds, and suddenly caught sight of a tiny dark speck down below, on the sea. She winked her eyes and stared hard, and it seemed to her that she saw a tiny sail go flap, flap and a tiny ship heading for the shore.

"Pirates! These must be pirates!" said the Moon. "Nobody else would be creeping into harbor at this hour!" And she called out to the clouds, "Move away, all of you, and give me a clear sky. I want to see what is going on here."

The clouds drifted away at once and the Moon turned her brightest light on sea and land.

She made out the little ship, which had now reached harbor.

Two little red gnomes had gone ashore and were making the ship fast. And as they tugged at the ropes they sang:

"Tight as tight, and fast as fast,
The Elfin ship is home at last,
With cargo from a fairy clime
For boys and girls at Christmas time."

"Hi there!" cried the Moon, "what are you doing? Not so fast, I say, not so fast! You are pirates, that's what you are—pirates! You had better be off at once."

But the little gnomes took no notice at all, and in a few moments a great crowd of them rushed ashore carrying all kinds of things, apples and oranges and nuts and candy and dolls and drums and books and boats and Teddy bears and popcorn balls and ——.

"Well, I declare," cried the Moon, and she was very much excited. "Did anybody ever see anything like that? Let me tell you this: I am going to turn my light off, every bit of it; then you will not be able to see and you will wish that you had gone away when you were told."

And she was about to turn her light off when one of the little gnomes looked up and said: "Dear Mistress Moon, why are you scolding us? If you are not careful you will bring people from their beds to see what is the matter."

"Dear me!" cried the Moon, "isn't that exactly what I want to do? Let me tell you, I don't mean to have any pirates landing here if I can help it!"

"We are not pirates," said the red gnome. "This is an Elfin ship and her crew is made up of Mistletoe Mates and Holly Captains who are bringing a cargo of fairy gifts from fairyland. You seem quite to have forgotten that this is Christmas time."

"Dear me, why didn't you say so at once, and save me all this bother," said the Moon; but her tone was kinder and she did not turn off her light. Before the gnome could reply she went on, rather grumblingly: "I don't see why you have so many captains. It's most unusual—most!"

"With a valuable cargo like ours you can't have too many captains," said the gnome. "Besides, every Holly Captain wants to sail with the Christmas cargo and you simply can't keep them out. Let me tell you this—*I* am a Holly Captain!" With that he returned to his work and the Moon, who was now in quite a good humor, shed her brightest smile while the Christmas cargo was brought to land.

THE SNOWFLAKE

A snowflake set out on its journey from the sky to the earth. Hundreds of others were traveling at the same time, but he was the biggest of them all. When now and then a gleam of sunlight caught him he flashed and sparkled as if he had been made of diamonds. Gently and silently he fell through the crisp, cold air. But by and by a great wind swept up and set the snowflakes twisting and twirling and dancing till they were all caught in its mighty current and went streaming in one direction.

"Where are you taking me?" said the snowflake to the wind. But the wind did not answer.

Out just below them was a big town, with many houses and tall chimneys from which rolled fold after fold of black smoke.

"Don't take me there," said the snowflake. "Please leave me among the buttercups in the field."

But the wind did not answer. Swifter and swifter the snowflake fell. Now it was over the roofs of the houses.

Soon it was flying away among the muddy streets. Then a gust of wind swept it over a wall into a back garden. There was no grass there. It was covered with cinders, fish bones, broken jugs, bottles, and battered tins. The snowflake fell between two empty, rusty sardine tins and lay still.

"Think of bringing me to this untidy back yard." And he began to cry, and cried so much that he cried himself away.

Now just where the snowflake fell two little seeds had been trying to grow. They had put forth roots and little green heads and then had stopped because they could not get any moisture. They were very, very near death when that little snowflake came with its drop of water and saved them.

In spring two lovely little flowers waved their snowy plumes in that back yard. And one morning a woman who saw them picked them and carried them to her little sick boy and set them in a glass by his bed. Every time he looked at them his eyes gleamed and his lips smiled, for they made his little heart full of joy.

THE BIRDIES' BREAKFAST

Two little birdies, one wintry day,
Began to wonder, and then to say,
"How about breakfast, this wintry day?"

Two little maidens, one wintry day,
Into the garden wended their way
Where the snow lay deep, that wintry day.

One, with a broom, swept the snow away;
One scattered crumbs, then away to play.
And the birdies had breakfast that wintry day.

FOR THE READING HOUR

THE BASKET OF BULRUSHES

Now there was a great famine in the land of Canaan and many of the Children of Israel, with their flocks and herds and all that they had, left their homes and went down into Egypt.

Pharaoh, the king, welcomed these strangers and he commanded that the best of the land should be theirs.

While the good king lived the Children of Israel were very happy. But at last he died and a second Pharaoh ruled over Egypt. He knew that the Children of Israel had come from a country far away. He knew, too, that while they had lived in his country, they had grown to be a splendid people. They loved and worshipped their God and tried to be good. But Pharaoh did not wish them to be in Egypt. He feared their growing strength.

And one day Pharaoh said to his people: "The Children of Israel are more and mightier than we are. Come, let us deal wisely with them. If we do not, they may join themselves to our enemies and fight against us."

So the cruel king set taskmasters over the Children of Israel, and they were made to work very hard. They had to dig up clay, make bricks and dry them, then carry their heavy loads in the hot sun. In this way were the lives of these people made bitter in hard bondage and with all manner of hard tasks.

But the more the king made them work the more there were of them, men, women, and children. For they were a mighty people who loved their God. Then the king became angry and charged all his people, saying:

"Every son that is born to these people ye shall cast into the river. But every daughter ye shall save alive."

Now there was a very good woman of the Children of Israel who had a little baby boy. And when she saw that he was a goodly child she hid him for three months so that the king's men could not find him. And she prayed to God to watch over her child.

But a time came when she could hide the babe no longer. So she made for him a basket of bulrushes. This she daubed with slime and pitch that no water could get in. She put the babe inside the basket and laid it in the flags by the river's brink. And the babe's sister, Miriam, stood afar off to see what would become of her little brother.

Soon the king's daughter, the princess, with her hand-maidens, came down to bathe at the river. As the princess was walking along by the water's edge, she saw the little basket lying among the flags.

"Fetch it to me," she said to one of her handmaidens.

The maiden obeyed. When the princess opened the basket she found the goodly babe lying in it. And behold, the child wept and the princess had pity on it.

"Surely, this is a babe of one of the Children of Israel," she said, "I will keep him for my own."

Then Miriam, who had been watching from afar off, came near. When she saw that the princess pitied the babe she said to her:

"Shall I go and call a nurse that she may nurse the babe for thee?"

"Go," said the princess. And Miriam went and called the babe's own mother.

Now when the princess saw the woman, she said:

"Take this child and nurse it." And the mother knew that her prayers had been answered.

The babe grew, and his mother brought him unto Pharaoh's daughter, the princess, and he became her son. And she called his name Moses.

BECKY'S CHRISTMAS DREAM

All alone by the kitchen fire sat little Becky. Every one else had gone away to keep Christmas and left her to take care of the house. Nobody had thought to give her any presents, or take her to any merrymaking.

This little girl was from the poorhouse. She was twelve years old but she was bound to work for the farmer's wife until she was eighteen. She had no father or mother, no friend or home but this. As she sat alone by the fire her little heart ached for some one to love and cherish her.

Becky was a shy, quiet child, with a thin face and eyes that always seemed trying to find something that she wanted to find very much. She worked away, day after day, so patiently and silently that no one ever guessed what curious thoughts filled the little cropped head, or what a tender child's heart was hidden under the blue-checked pinafore.

To-night she was wishing that there were fairies in the world, who would whisk down the chimney and give her many pretty things, as they did in the delightful fairy tales.

"I am sure I am as poor and lonely as Cinderella. I need a kind godmother to help me as much as ever she did," said Becky to herself. She sat on her little stool staring at the fire, which didn't burn very well, for she felt too much out of sorts to care whether things looked cheerful or not.

There is an old belief that all dumb things can speak for one hour on Christmas Eve. Now, Becky knew nothing of this story and no one can say whether what happened was true or whether she fell asleep and dreamed it. But certain it is when Becky spoke about Cinderella she was amazed to hear a small voice reply:

"Well, my dear, I shall be very glad to give you some advice. I've had much experience in this world."

Becky stared about her, but all she saw was the old gray cat, blinking at the fire.

"Did you speak, Tabby?" said the child, at last.

"Of course I did. If you wish a godmother, here I am."

Becky laughed at the idea; but Puss, with her silver-gray suit, white handkerchief crossed on her bosom, kind, motherly old face, and cozy purr, did make a very good little godmother after all.

"Well, ma'am, I'm ready to listen," said Becky.

"First, my child, what do you want most?" asked the godmother, quite in the fairy-book style.

"To be loved by everybody," answered Becky.

"Good," said the cat. "I'm pleased with that answer; it's sensible, and I'll tell you how to get your wish. Learn to make people love you by loving them."

"I don't know how," sighed Becky.

"No more did I, in the beginning," returned Puss gently. "When I first came here, a shy young kitten, I thought only of keeping out of everybody's way, for I was afraid of every one. I hid under the barn and came out only when no one was near. I wasn't happy, for I wanted to be petted, but didn't know how to begin. One day I heard Aunt Sally say to the master, 'James, that wild kitten isn't any use at all, you had better drown her and get a nice tame one to amuse the children and clear the house of mice.' 'The poor thing has been abused, I guess, so we will give her another trial and maybe she will come to trust us after a while,' said the good master. I thought over these things as I lay under the barn, and resolved to do my best, for I did not want to be drowned. It was hard at first, but I began by coming out when little Jane called me and letting her play with me. Then I ventured into the house, and finding a welcome at my first visit, I went again and took a mouse with me to show that I wasn't idle. No one hurt or frightened me, and soon I was the household pet. For several years I have led a happy life here."

Becky listened eagerly, and when Puss had ended she said timidly, "Do you think if I try not to be afraid, but to show that I want to be affectionate, the people will let me and will like it?"

"Very sure. I heard the mistress say you were a good handy little thing. Do as I did, my dear, and you will find that there is plenty of love in the world."

"I will. Thank you, dear old Puss, for your advice."

Puss came to rub her soft cheek against Becky's hand, and then settled herself in a cozy hunch in Becky's lap. Presently another voice spoke, a queer, monotonous voice, high above her.

"Tick, tick; wish again, little Becky, and I'll tell you how to find your wish." It was the old moon-faced clock behind the door, which had struck twelve just before Tabby first spoke.

"Dear me," said Becky, "how queerly things do act to-night!" She thought a moment, then said soberly, "I wish I liked my work better. Washing dishes, picking chips, and hemming towels is such tiresome work. I don't see how I *can* go on doing it for six more years."

"Just what I used to feel," said the clock. "I couldn't bear to think that I had to stand here and do nothing but tick year after year. I flatly said I wouldn't, and I stopped a dozen times a day. Bless me, what a fuss I made until I was put in this corner to stand idle for several months. At first I rejoiced, then I grew tired of doing nothing, and began to reflect that as I was born a clock, it would be wiser to do my duty and get some satisfaction out of it if I could."

"And so you began to go again? Please teach me to be faithful and to love my duty," cried Becky.

"I will"; and the old clock grandly struck the half hour, with a smile on its round face, as it steadily ticked on.

Here the fire blazed up and the teakettle hanging on the crane began to sing.

"How cheerful that is," said Becky, as the whole kitchen brightened with the ruddy glow. "If I could have a third wish, I'd wish to be as cheerful as the fire."

"Have your wish if you choose, but you must work for it, as I do," cried the fire, as its flames embraced the old kettle till it gurgled with pleasure.

Becky thought she heard a queer voice humming these words:

> "I'm an old black kettle
> With a very crooked nose,
> But I can't help being gay
> When the jolly fire glows."

"I shouldn't wonder a mite if that child had been up to mischief to-night, rummaged all over the house, eaten herself sick, or stolen something and run away with it," fretted Aunt Sally, as the family went jingling home in the big sleigh about one o'clock from the Christmas party.

"Tut, tut, Aunty, I wouldn't think evil of the poor little thing. If I'd had my way she would have gone with us and had a good time. She doesn't look as if she had seen many, and I have a notion it is what she needs," said the farmer kindly.

"The thought of her alone at home has worried me all the evening, but she didn't seem to mind, and I haven't had time to get a respectable dress ready for her to wear, so I let it go," added the farmer's wife, as she cuddled little Jane under the cloaks and shawls, with a regretful memory of Becky knocking at her heart.

"I have some popcorn and a bouncing big apple for her," said Billy, the red-faced lad perched up by his father playing driver.

"And I'll give her one of my dolls. She said she never had one. Wasn't that dreadful?" put in little Jane, popping out her head like a bird from its nest.

"Better see what she has been doing first," advised Aunt Sally. "If she hasn't done any mischief and has remembered to have the kettle boiling so I can have a cup of hot tea after my ride, and if she has kept the fire up and warmed my slippers, I don't know but I'll give her the red mittens I knit."

They found Becky lying on the bare floor, her head pillowed on the stool, and old Tabby in her arms, with a

The moon was sailing out from the clouds.
Page 189

The Reading Hour
Page 195

corner of the blue pinafore spread over her. The fire was burning splendidly, the kettle simmering, and in a row upon the hearth stood not only Aunt Sally's old slippers, but those of master and mistress also, and over a chair hung two little nightgowns warming for the children.

"Well, now, who could have been more thoughtful than that!" said Aunt Sally. "Becky shall have those mittens, and I'll knit her two pairs of stockings—that I will."

So Aunt Sally laid the gay mittens close to the little rough hand that had worked so busily all day. Billy set his big red apple and bag of popcorn just where she would see them when she awoke. Jane laid the doll in Becky's arms, and Tabby smelled of it approvingly, to the children's delight. The farmer had no present ready, but he stroked the little cropped head with a fatherly touch that made Becky smile in her sleep, as he said within himself, "I will do by this forlorn child as I would wish any one to do by my Janey if she were left alone."

But the mother gave the best gift of all, for she stooped down and kissed Becky as only a mother can kiss. The good woman's heart reproached her for neglect of the child who had no mother.

That unusual touch awakened Becky at once, and looking about her with astonished eyes, she saw such a wonderful change in all the faces that she clapped her hands and cried with a happy laugh, "My dream's come true! Oh, my dream's come true!"

Used by permission of John S. P. Alcott.

A GARDEN SURPRISE

When George Washington was a little boy he was much surprised one spring day at something which he saw in the garden. He found that the cabbage bed had begun to show green shoots, and that the green formed the letters of his own name, *George Washington*. He stood for a few moments quite silent, his eyes and mouth wide open in astonishment. Surely it must be magic!

"Father, father," he shouted; "O father, do come and see."

"What is it?" asked his father.

"The cabbages are coming up, and are writing out my name."

"Very curious," said his father.

"But who did it?" asked George.

"Do you think they come up that way by chance?" asked his father.

"They couldn't," said George. "Cabbages couldn't grow that way unless some one had planted them so."

"You are quite right," said his father. "Nothing grows by chance. I planted those cabbages in that way on purpose to teach you that very lesson, my boy. There are some people who think that everything grows by chance, but that is impossible. There is some one who plans everything. All the thousands of good things you enjoy, the sunshine and the flowers, eyes to see with, ears to hear with, feet to carry you about, all are planned by God, and not by chance."

George was only eight years old when he learned this lesson, but he never forgot it all his life.

A TRUTHFUL LAD

When George Washington was about six years old his father gave him a little hatchet. Like most boys of his age he was very proud of his gift. He was constantly going about chopping everything that came in his way.

One day while he was in the garden he tried the edge of his hatchet on the trunk of a beautiful young cherry tree. So terribly did he injure the tree that it soon died.

When at last George's father discovered what had happened to his tree he went immediately into the house and asked who had done the mischief.

"I would not have taken anything for that tree," he exclaimed.

No one could tell him anything about it.

Presently, George with his hatchet, came running into the house.

"George," said his father, "do you know who killed that beautiful little cherry tree in the garden?"

Looking at his father, George said bravely: "I did, father. I cut it with my little hatchet."

"My boy," said his father after a few moments, "I am sorry, indeed, to have lost my tree, but glad I am that you have told me the truth. I would rather lose every tree in my orchard than have my boy tell a lie."

CHRISTMAS GIFTS

"Mother," said Jack, "may I have some money to buy Christmas presents with?"

"Dear," said his mother, "I have no money. We are very poor, and I can hardly buy enough food for us all."

Jack hung his head.

"All the other boys give presents!" he said.

"So shall you!" said his mother. "All presents are not bought with money."

So his mother told him this and that; and soon after Jack started out, dressed in his best suit, to give his presents.

First, he went to Aunt Jane's house. She was old and lame, and she did not like boys.

"What do you want?" she asked.

"Merry Christmas!" said Jack. "May I stay for an hour and help you?"

"Humph!" said Aunt Jane. "Want to keep you out of mischief, do they? Well, you may bring in some wood."

"Shall I split some kindling, too?" asked Jack.

"If you know how," said Aunt Jane. "I can't have you cutting your foot and messing my clean shed all up."

Jack found some fresh pine wood and a bright hatchet, and he split up a great pile of kindling and thought it fun. He stacked it neatly, and then brought in a pail of fresh water and filled the kettle.

"What else can I do?" he asked. "There are twenty minutes more."

"Humph!" said Aunt Jane. "You might feed the pig."

Jack fed the pig, who thanked him in his own way.

"Ten minutes more!" he said. "What shall I do now?"

"Humph!" said Aunt Jane. "You may sit down and tell me why you came."

"It is a Christmas present!" said Jack. "I am giving hours for presents. I had twelve—but I gave one to mother, and another one was gone before I knew I had it. This hour was your present."

"Humph!" said Aunt Jane. She hobbled to the cupboard and took out a small round pie that smelt very good. "Here!" she said. "This is *your* present, and I thank you for mine. Come again, will you?"

"Indeed I will," said Jack, "and thank you for the pie!"

Next Jack went and read for an hour to old Mr. Green, who was blind. He read a book about the sea, and they both liked it very much, so the hour went quickly. Then it was time to help mother get dinner, and then time to eat it; that took two hours, and Aunt Jane's pie was wonderful. Then Jack took the Smith baby for a ride in its carriage, as Mrs. Smith was ill, and they met its grandfather, who filled Jack's pockets with candy and popcorn and invited him to a Christmas tree that night.

Next Jack went to see Willy Brown, who had been ill for a long time and could not leave his bed. Willy was very glad to see him; they played a game, and then each told the other a story, and before Jack knew it the clock struck six.

"Oh!" cried Jack. "You have had two!"

"Two what?" asked Willy.

"Two hours!" said Jack; and he told Willy about the presents he was giving. "I am glad I gave you two," he said, "and I would give you three, but I must go and help mother."

"Oh, dear!" said Willy. "I thank you very much, Jack.

I have had a perfectly great time; but I have nothing to give you."

Jack laughed. "Why, don't you see?" he cried; "you have given me just the same thing. I have had a great time, too."

"Mother," said Jack, as he was going to bed, "I have had a splendid Christmas, but I wish I had had something to give you besides the hours."

"My darling," said his mother, "you have given me the best gift of all—yourself!"

THE SELFISH GIANT

Every afternoon, as they were coming from school, the children used to go and play in the Giant's garden.

It was a large lovely garden, with soft green grass. Here and there over the grass stood beautiful flowers like stars, and there were twelve peach trees that in the springtime broke out into delicate blossoms of pink and pearl, and in the autumn bore rich fruit. The birds sat on the trees and sang so sweetly that the children used to stop their games in order to listen to them. "How happy we are here!" they cried to one another.

One day the Giant came back. He had been to visit his friend the Ogre and had stayed with him for seven years. When he arrived he saw the children playing in the garden.

"What are you doing there?" he cried in a very gruff voice, and the children ran away.

"My own garden is my own garden," said the Giant; "I will allow nobody to play in it but myself." So he built a high wall all around it, and put up a notice-board—

KEEP OUT
OF
THIS GARDEN

He was a very selfish giant.

The poor children had nowhere to play. They tried to play on the road, but the road was very dusty and full of hard stones, and they did not like it. They used to wander round the high wall when their lessons were over, and talk about the beautiful garden inside.

"How happy we were there," they said to one another.

Then the Spring came, and all over the country there were little blossoms and little birds.

But in the garden of the Selfish Giant it was still winter. The birds did not care to sing in it, as there were no children, and the trees forgot to blossom. Once a beautiful flower put its head out from the grass, and when it saw the notice-board it was so sorry for the children that it slipped back into the ground again, and went off to sleep. The only people who were pleased were the Snow and the Frost.

"Spring has forgotten this garden," they cried, "so we will live here all the year around."

The Snow covered up the grass with her great white cloak, and the Frost painted all the trees silver. Then they invited the North Wind to stay with them, and he came. He was wrapped in furs, and he roared all day about the garden, and blew the chimney-pots down.

"This is a delightful spot," he said; "we must ask the Hail on a visit." So the Hail came. Every day for three hours he rattled on the roof of the castle till he broke most of the slates, and then he ran round and round the garden as fast as he could go. He was dressed in gray and his breath was like ice.

"I cannot understand why the Spring is so late in coming," said the Selfish Giant, as he sat at the window and looked out at his cold white garden; "I hope there will be a change in the weather."

But the Spring never came, nor the Summer. The Autumn gave golden fruit to every garden, but to the Giant's garden she gave none.

"He is too selfish," she said. So it was always Winter there and the North Wind and the Hail and the Frost and the Snow danced about through the trees.

One morning the Giant was lying awake on his bed

when he heard some lovely music. It sounded so sweet to his ears that he thought it must be the King's musicians passing by. It was really only a little linnet singing outside his window, but it was so long since he had heard a bird sing in his garden that it seemed to him to be the most beautiful music in the world.

Then the Hail stopped dancing over his head, and the North Wind ceased roaring, and a delicious perfume came to him through the open casement. "I believe the Spring has come at last," said the Giant, and he jumped out of bed and looked out.

What did he see?

He saw a most wonderful sight. Through a little hole in the wall the children had crept in, and they were sitting in the branches of the trees. In every tree that he could see there was a little child. And the trees were so glad to have the children back again that they had covered themselves with blossoms, and were waving their arms gently above the children's heads. The birds were flying about and twittering with delight, and the flowers were looking up through the green grass and laughing. It was a lovely scene, only in one corner it was still winter. It was the farthest corner of the garden, and in it was standing a little boy. He was so small that he could not reach up to the branches of the tree, and he was wandering all round it, crying bitterly. The poor tree was still quite covered with frost and snow, and the North Wind was blowing and roaring above it.

"Climb up! little boy," said the Tree, and it bent its branches down as low as it could; but the boy was too tiny.

And the Giant's heart melted as he looked out. "How selfish I have been!" he said; "now I know why the Spring would not come here. I will put that poor little boy on the top of the tree, and then I will knock down the wall, and my garden shall be the children's playground forever and ever." He was really very sorry for what he had done.

So he crept downstairs and opened the front door quite softly, and went out into the garden. But when the children saw him they were so frightened that they all ran away, and the garden became winter again. Only the little boy did not run, for his eyes were so full of tears that he did not see the Giant coming.

And the Giant strode up behind him and took him gently in his hand, and put him up into the tree. And the tree broke at once into blossoms, and the birds came and sang on it, and the little boy stretched out his two arms and flung them round the Giant's neck, and kissed him. And the other children, when they saw that the Giant was not wicked any longer, came running back, and with them came the Spring.

"It is your garden now, little children," said the Giant, and he took a great axe and knocked down the wall.

And when the people were going to market at twelve o'clock they found the Giant playing with the children in the most beautiful garden they had ever seen.

A LITTLE NURSE

There was once a little girl named Florence Nightingale. She lived across the sea in a country called England.

When she was a very little girl she showed a great love for people and animals. She even made friends with the shy squirrels. When any one was ill Florence would act as nurse and do everything she could to relieve pain.

Near the village where this little girl's home was, lived an old shepherd named Roger. He had a favorite sheep dog that he called Cap, of whom Florence was very fond.

Roger and Cap were the best of friends; in fact Cap was Roger's only companion. The dog helped his master to look after the sheep by day and kept him company at night.

Cap was a fine sheep dog. He looked after the flocks with such care that old Roger had to trouble little about them.

One day Florence was riding out with a friend. She saw Roger feeding his sheep, but Cap was not helping him. The sheep, too, missed Cap's watching, for they were scampering about in all directions.

Florence stopped to ask her old friend what had become of Cap.

"Alas, my dear friend," said old Roger, "Cap will never help take care of my sheep again. A mischievous school boy threw a stone at him yesterday and broke one of his legs. I shall have to put him out of his misery."

The old shepherd wiped away tears which filled his eyes.

"My poor Cap," was all he said.

Little Florence was very sad when she heard this.

"Are you sure his leg is broken?" she asked.

"O, yes, Miss Florence. He has not put his foot on the ground since the stone struck him; and he is in great pain."

"Let us go to see Cap," said Florence to her companion. "The leg may not be really broken. It would take a big stone to break the leg of a dog like Cap."

On the two rode until they reached the old shepherd's cottage. There on the floor lay poor Cap in great pain.

At first he would not let the little girl touch him. But

she spoke to him kindly. Then he let her take his injured leg in her hand.

She found the leg much hurt and it was badly swollen; but it was not broken.

"Cap will come around all right if he has rest," said Florence's companion.

"How glad I am," she said. "Can't we do something to relieve his suffering? He seems in such pain."

"Bathe the leg in hot water. That will soon ease the pain and will help to cure him, too," was her companion's advice.

The little nurse lighted a fire. Then she found some strips of old flannel. These she dipped into hot water, then wrung them out and laid them on the bruises.

Poor Cap moaned and winced with pain, but he seemed to know that Florence was doing everything to relieve his sufferings. At last he licked her hands and wagged his tail to show her how thankful he was.

On their way home they met old Roger.

"O, Roger," cried Florence, "your dog's leg is not broken. I have bandaged it with flannel. Don't kill him. I'm sure he will be well again in a few days."

"I am thankful to hear that," said old Roger, "and grateful to you, child, for what you have done to save my Cap."

The next morning Florence went to see the dog again. Cap came up to her, for he knew she was his friend. She bathed the leg once more and bound it up.

In a few days Cap was able to run about the meadows and help Roger take care of the sheep.

After that Cap always ran to Florence when she came to see him. He would jump about to show her that he was well again and happy.

"If it had not been for your kindness," said old Roger one day to Florence, "I would have killed the best dog in the world."

This little girl grew to be a kind and useful woman. At one time when a terrible war was going on in a far country she left her home and went to the place of battle. She took care of sick and wounded soldiers.

Her untiring work there saved many, many lives. To this day people honor the name of this kind and helpful woman—Florence Nightingale.

MOTHER'S CHRISTMAS PRESENT

Once upon a time, just before Christmas, everybody at Polly's home was making Christmas presents. Mother was crocheting grandmother a shawl; Father was making a set of bookshelves for Brother Tom; and Tom was hammering away on something that he would not let Polly see.

"I wish I could make a Christmas present, too," said Polly, who was only six years old.

"Why, you can," said grandmother, putting her knitting down and smiling at the little girl. "When I was just your age I made a needlebook for my mother's Christmas present. It had blue satin backs and two flannel leaves. Would you like to make your mother one?"

"Oh, yes, yes," said Polly; and she was so pleased that she hugged grandmother, and then ran all the way downstairs to hug mother, too.

She did not tell mother about the needlebook. No, indeed, though it was so hard for her to keep a secret that she

227

put her hand over her mouth and hurried back to grandmother's room as fast as she could for fear it would slip off the tip of her tongue in spite of all she could do.

Grandmother had some bits of white flannel and blue satin in her scrap bag, and the needlebook was begun at once. First the leaves had to be cut just the right shape and size. Then Polly threaded her needle with pretty blue thread, and grandmother showed her how to sew over and over the edges of the flannel to keep it from raveling. It took a long time to do this but a Christmas present cannot be made in a hurry—not if you take as much pains with it as Polly did. Sometimes, it is true, her thread got tangled, sometimes her fingers grew tired, and sometimes her stitches were so uneven that she had to take them out and do them over again; but she kept trying and trying till at last grandmother said she could not have done better work herself, when she was a little girl.

Polly finished the leaves for the needlework on the very afternoon before Christmas and grandmother was just telling her how to make the backs for it when Uncle John drove up to the house with a fine new sleigh and tinkling bells.

"Pollikins! Pollikins," he called, and Polly knew what he wanted as soon as she heard him.

"Uncle John has come to take me for a sleigh ride," she cried in delight; and she dropped her scissors and satin and flannel all in a heap and started to the nursery for her hood and cloak.

"But what will you do about your mother's Christmas present if you go sleighing?" asked grandmother, just as she got to the door.

"Oh!" said Polly, stopping short. "Oh!"

"If you want to put it on the breakfast table with all the rest of her presents, it will have to be finished to-day," said grandmother.

"I could finish it when I came home," said Polly, and her voice sounded as if she were about to cry.

"Perhaps you could, but perhaps you could not. Think how long it took you to make the leaves," said grandmother.

"Come on," called Uncle John.

Tinkle, tink, rang the sleigh bells.

Dear me, what was a little girl to do! Polly looked at grandmother, and the little heap of work and out of the window at Uncle John; and then, what do you think she did?

Went sleighing? No, when Uncle John drove away in his fine new sleigh with tinkling bells, no little girl named Polly sat beside him. She was in grandmother's room sewing as fast as her needle could fly.

And when mother came down to breakfast on Christmas morning the first thing she spied on the table was the needlebook. And, oh, how pleased she was!

"I love every stitch in it," she said. "It is the dearest Christmas present I have ever had."

Polly had Christmas presents, too. Santa Claus had brought her a doll; Brother Tom had made her a doll house, and mother, father, and grandmother each had a gift for her; but I really believe the present she enjoyed most was the one she made herself and gave to her mother.

BENNIE'S SUNSHINE

Little Bennie lived with his grandmother, in the basement of an old house. The street was so narrow that the warm sunlight could not shine into the low rooms, and grandmother was too feeble to go out of doors. She had been sick now for a week, and a kind neighbor came in to help with the work. Little Ben did errands, and tried his best to be useful.

It was a pleasant spring day, and after Bennie had come from the store with a pitcher of milk, he sat by grandmother's bed, and told her how warm and bright the sunshine was, and how he wished it would shine into their windows. "Ah! it has been so long since I felt the sunshine!" cried grandmother, and she sighed. While Bennie watched her she seemed to sleep, and he put on his cap, poured the milk into a bowl, and went out, with the pitcher in his hand, shutting the door softly behind him. He had a plan for bringing sunshine to dear grandmother. Was not the Common near, where the sun just shines all day long? Surely some of it could be spared for her.

So little Ben ran all the way, till he came to the wide Common. Then he placed the pitcher carefully down on the grass, so the sun could shine straight into it. "I will wait till it is quite full," he thought. Then he began to pick the yellow buttercups that grew all about. He soon had a big bunch, and they were as bright as the sunshine. "Grandma will be so surprised when she wakes up, and how pleased she will be to have the sunshine, after all," Bennie thought. He started for home, with the buttercups in one hand and the pitcher in the other, his face rosy and smiling.

Grandmother was still asleep, so he laid the buttercups on her pillow, where she would be sure to see them, as soon as she opened her eyes. He set the pitcher on the table, and sang:

> "Wake! says the Sunshine,
>   'Tis time to get up;
> Wake! pretty daisy,
>   And sweet buttercup."

Soon she opened her eyes, and the first thing she saw was the bunch of buttercups.

"Why, they are like sunshine!" she said.

"Yes, grandmother," cried little Ben, "and I have filled the pitcher with real sunshine—just see!" But when they looked inside, the pitcher was empty; all the bright light had gone out of it.

Grandmother comforted her dear little boy by telling him that the buttercups and his loving face were sunshine to her; if she could not go into the beautiful country, she was happy with him always.

It was not long after this that kind friends came and took little Ben and his grandmother out into the country, to stay all summer. And with the sunshine and little Ben to help her, grandmother at last grew strong enough to walk in the green fields. She called Bennie "Little Sunshine." Don't you think it was a good name for him?

THE OGRE THAT PLAYED
JACKSTRAWS

Once there was a giant **Ogre** who lived in a huge castle that was built right in the middle of a valley. All men had to pass this castle on their way to the king's palace, which stood on a rock at the head of the valley.

They were all afraid of the **Ogre** and ran just as fast as they could when they went by. And when they looked back, they could see the **Ogre** sitting on the wall of his castle, scowling at them very fiercely.

He had a head as large as a barrel, with great black eyes and long, bushy eyelashes. When he opened his mouth, they saw that it was full of teeth, and so they ran away faster than ever, without caring to see anything more.

The king wanted to get rid of the **Ogre**; so he sent his men to drive him away and to tear down his castle. But the Ogre scowled at them so savagely that their teeth began to fall out, and they all turned back and said they dared not fight such a horrid creature.

Then Roger, the king's son, rode his black horse, Hurricane, up to the door of the Ogre's castle, and struck hard against the door with his iron glove.

The door opened and out came the Ogre. He seized Roger in one hand and the great black horse in the other, and rubbed their heads together; and while he did this, he made them very small.

Then he tumbled them over the wall into his garden. They crawled through a hole in the garden fence and both ran home,—Roger one way and Hurricane the other. Neither of them dared to tell the king or anyone else where he had been, or what the Ogre had done to him. But it was two or three days before they became large again.

Then the king sent out some men with a cannon to batter down the walls of the Ogre's castle. But the Ogre sat on the wall and caught the cannon balls in his hand and tossed them back at the cannon, so that they broke the wheels and scared away all the men.

When the cannon sounded, the Ogre roared so loudly that every window in the king's palace was broken. The queen and all her princesses went down into the cellar, where they hid among the sugar barrels, and stuffed cotton in their ears till the noise should stop.

Whatever the king's men tried to do, the Ogre made it worse and worse, so that at last no one dared to go out into the valley beside the Ogre's castle. No one dared to look at the castle from anywhere, because, when the Ogre scowled, all who saw him dropped to the ground with fear, and their teeth began to fall out. And when the Ogre roared, there was no one who could bear to hear it.

So the king and all his men hid in the cellar of the castle with the queen and the princesses, and they stuffed their ears full of cotton, while the Ogre scowled and roared and had his own way.

But there was a little boy named Pennyroyal, who tended the black horse Hurricane. He was not afraid of anything because he was a little boy. This little boy said he would go out and see the Ogre and tell him to go away. The people were all so afraid that they could not ask Pennyroyal not to go. So he put on his hat, filled his pockets with marbles, took his kite under his arm, and went down the valley to the castle of the Ogre.

The Ogre sat on the wall and looked at him, but the little

boy was not afraid, and so it did the Ogre no good to scowl. Then Pennyroyal knocked on the Ogre's door and the Ogre opened it and looked at the little boy.

"Please, Mr. Ogre, may I come in?" said Pennyroyal.

Then the Ogre let the little boy in, and he began to walk around the castle, looking at all the things. There was one room filled with bones, but the Ogre was ashamed of it, and did not want the little boy to see it. So, when Pennyroyal was not looking, the Ogre changed the room and made it small, so that instead of a room full of bones it became just a box of jackstraws. And the big elephant which he kept there to play with, he made into a lap elephant, and the little boy took it in his hand and stroked its tiny tusks and tied a knot in its trunk. Everything that could frighten the little boy the Ogre made small and pretty.

By and by the Ogre himself grew smaller and smaller. He took off his ugly old face, with the long teeth and bushy eyelashes, and dropped it on the floor and covered it with a wolf-skin. Then he sat down on the wolf-skin, and the little boy sat down on the floor beside him, and they began to play a game with the box of jackstraws that had been a room full of bones. The Ogre had never been a boy himself, so jackstraws was the only game he knew how to play.

Then the elephant which the Ogre had made small snuggled down between them on the floor. And as they played with each other, the castle itself grew small, and shrank away until there was just room enough for them to play their game.

Up in the palace, when the Ogre stopped roaring, the king's men looked out and saw that the huge castle was gone. Then Roger, the king's son, called for Pennyroyal. But when he could not find the boy, he saddled the black horse Hurricane himself, and rode down the valley to the place where the Ogre's castle had been.

When he came back, he told the king that the Ogre and his castle were gone. Where the castle had stood there was nothing left but a board tent under an oak tree, and in the tent there were two little boys playing jackstraws, and between them on the ground lay a candy elephant.

That was all. For the terrible Ogre was the kind of ogre that treats people just exactly as they treat him. There isn't any other kind of Ogre.